HUSTLE

SAM JD HUNT

HUSTLE

A Sam's Town Novella

SAM JD HUNT

Follow Sam JD Hunt

Point your smartphone camera at the QR code above

Or visit: linktr.ee/samjdhunt

Point your phone's camera at the QR code.

"Do or do not. There is no try."
— Yoda, *Star Wars Episode V, The Empire Strikes Back*

"Redemption *always* demands sacrifice."
— Shane MacKinnon

"It's a great advantage not to drink among hard-drinking people."
— F. Scott Fitzgerald, *The Great Gatsby*

HUSTLE is even better after reading REDEMPTION & SACRIFICE

Contents

Shawn "Mack" MacKenzie was on the path to redemption, finally making the sacrifice necessary to overcome his criminal past.

But when a nemesis in blue condemns him to do the unthinkable, will he be able to navigate the dark world of the cuffed and the pinched?

Can Mack pull off the ultimate hustle in time to get back to Grace, love, and Sam's Town?

Find out in this sizzling spin-off of the hit *Sam's Town* Series.

Chapter One

MORMONS AND SOLAR SALES

I t started as it always did – with a knock on my shitty trailer door.

I ignored it.

"Mormons and solar sales," I muttered to my gorgeous girl in the kitchen. "That's all it ever is."

Her bluer-than-the-Mojave-sky-at-sunrise eyes glared at me. She was annoyed at the noise.

"No," I answered, the word a mere reflex to her constant demands.

The knock returned. She pointed at my rickety door, the gesture a clear command.

"It's no one. Finish up that drink, baby girl. We need to hustle."

She was the love of my life, but high maintenance as fuck.

Pointing again, she slammed her fist down. Patient she was not.

"Fine," I barked. It had already been a rough morning.

I opened the door as I reached for a shirt. That day in Vegas it was north of a hundred and ten degrees, and clothes weren't high on my priority list. Still, I didn't want to terrify the Jehovah's Witnesses I expected on the other side.

Okay, that's a lie. I totally wanted my gangster tattoo laden body to make them sweat through their polyester leggings.

"Did you bring my fuckin' heroin?" I growled, channeling my best inner thug as I flung open the door.

Big mistake.

"I forgot the heroin, but may I come in?"

Dammit.

The cop on my dusty porch gestured toward the dark room behind me. "We need to talk, MacKenzie."

"You got a warrant?" I tossed the t-shirt to the ground. I was far more intimidating with all my guns showing, including the Glock in the waistband of my jeans.

"C'mon, Mack, it's hotter than a tourist frying in the Vdara Death Ray out here."

If you lived in the Nevada desert, every conversation began with a less-than-original commentary on how hot it was. The trailer I owned, eclipsed by the hulking carcass of the Sam's Town Gambling Hall, was in the suburbs of Las Vegas. Well, "suburbs" is a nice word for something beyond shitty, sort of like saying "affair" for fucking around.

"What do you want, Ava?" I could hear Grace getting pissed in the kitchen behind us. She didn't have much patience with other women coming around.

Officer Ava Greene, dressed in full Metro PD blues, let her hand rest on her belly. "I wanted to tell you I'm pregnant. Do you think it'll be a pristine cop like me or a murdering felon like you?"

Now Grace was really about to boil.

"Funny."

I knew the blast from my past on my doorstep wasn't with child – I hadn't touched Ava in years. Although, the last time we'd fornicated, it was in the back of a police car. *Her* police car. I shit you not.

"I figured maybe some of that leftover spunk from Sam's Town's legendary gangster-turned-legit-MMA trainer-baby-daddy might've knocked me up even twenty-seven months post-coitus." She chuckled – yes, chuckled – as if she were actually witty.

"You've got ten minutes for whatever bullshit you're here for. I've got to hustle today."

She nodded, a long chestnut wave of hair draping over her dark eyes.

Walking past me, she glanced around the tiny room.

"Yeah, I heard you were training Oliver Martinez for the fight of the century. Must be a nice gig. And yet, you're still slummin' here in your grandma's ancient trailer?"

"You can take the boy outta Sam's Town, I guess…" I muttered as a cup slammed into my back. My lady in the kitchen had a temper, that was for sure.

Ava ignored her jealous rival for my attention. "Well, Mack, I'll admit it took me a while to track you down today. Word on the street had you living the lux life out at Red Rock."

I walked over to the red-faced Grace in her highchair and lifted her into my arms. My daughter was my world and always came first.

"Yeah, well, we had to come back over because a certain little miss left Harold in her old nursery when we were here cleaning it out the other day," I explained.

Grace held the bear up to show Ava, although her death stare at the perceived intruder didn't waiver.

Ava leaned in toward Grace, then thought better of it and backed away. It was a good thing – that toddler bit

3

worse than an elderly Chihuahua surrounded by strangers' ankles.

"The bear's name is Winnie the Pooh, silly," Ava said to Grace in a ridiculous-as-fuck sing-song tone. I never understood why people thought they should talk to children as if they were idiots.

"H'wold!" Grace said with an I'll-cut-you sneer. She didn't suffer fools.

"She's definitely your mini-me," Ava said as she flopped into the threadbare sofa. "But listen, Mack, I'm not here for Daddy and Me hour. I need you to go blue one more time."

Go blue. Those words sent a chill down my spine despite the crackling summer heat.

"I'm never doing that again, Ava. Ever."

I'd done it once, but I was never going undercover for them again. As the former enforcer for the notorious Saints & Sinners gang, another round at the cop charade was a hard no for me. And this time, Officer Ava Greene wasn't going to convince me with a blowjob. Or twelve.

She took a deep breath and slowly let it out, as if preparing herself for battle. "You will."

Chapter Two

HOT FUSS

"It's too hot to fuss." Ava collapsed into the couch as if it were all too much.

We were about to spar, clearly, but we both needed a breather before things got medieval. What she wanted from me I'd never give, in more ways than one.

"That line is from *Gatsby*, right? What an epic read! The oppressive heat was a character of its own."

"Mack MacKenzie, The Literate Killer. Who knew?"

"Not much else to do year after year in prison. Thanks for always bringing me books, by the way. You know you were one of the few people who visited me after the first couple of months?"

"I saw your mom here that time you asked me to sneak you in your old Blackberry. She said something about it being too much to see you like that."

"Like that," I repeated with a shrug. "Funny how she had no problem seeing me break bones and sling smack. I guess that paid more than my unfortunate incarceration for her."

She sighed and glanced around. "I remember the last time I was sent to arrest you. Do you, Mack?"

I did.

Ava was from the same Sam's Town block as I was. We'd grown up together and had been friends once, and then more than friends. As we slid into our teens, I sold her drugs and she took them. One day she landed in rehab after a particularly hairy episode. After that, she cleaned up and went through the police academy.

That's when I cut her off completely. The young thug in me saw it as a betrayal. But one scorching summer afternoon years later, our paths slammed into each other. It was never more than physical between Ava and me, but back then the chemistry was pure combustion.

And since I'm new at this memoir writing thing, I should make some sort of disclaimer that the following is a flashback scene. I'm a lot of things, but a cheater is not one of them.

Ava's asshole superiors thought it would be entertaining to send her alone to bring me in for some bullshit that went down the night before. They knew we had history.

So there she'd stood on my doorstep that day years ago. The midday sun was so powerful that she glowed from behind like she was on fire.

She still looked good, I had to give her that.

"Traitor." That was all I had to say.

"I did what I needed to do. You can make this easy, or you can make this hard."

She clearly watched too much *Law & Order*. "You plan to make it hard, Ava?"

"Difficult. I meant…difficult." But she was flustered and more than once her lusty gaze drifted across my body.

"My eyes are up here, Officer Greene."

"Stop it, Mack! They already hate me. If I don't bring you in, they're just going to send in the team."

"Maybe I like *the team*. It'll look way more badass to the 'hood being hauled out of here all bloody with ten guys bashing me. Can't have public perception slipping, now can I?"

She walked right passed me and into my house that day, too.

"Ava, get the fuck out. You need a warrant. I think you suck at this police thing."

But as I turned, she'd managed to get one handcuff around my thick left wrist.

She wasn't bad at her stuff, I'd give her that. Of course, I was better.

Cuffs were fun. And although I didn't much use them for "work" back then, I certainly used them regularly for play.

She hadn't counted on my wrist being so big, however. *Rookie mistake.*

It hadn't quite latched, and it took one quick turn to gain control of the cuffs. Within seconds, her own lovely wrists were bound behind her.

"Nice bracelets."

"Dammit, Mack! Let me go. I worked fucking hard to learn this shit."

"And I'm sure you're great at it. But this afternoon, you'll be great at being cuffed underneath me."

She writhed against the metal on her wrists in a useless attempt at turning the tables.

With a palm to her chest, I pushed her to the couch. "This might take a while, a citizen's arrest like this." My index finger traced the line between her overflowing breasts.

"You're the one under arrest, MacKenzie," she said

with a sharp inhale. "But it's my lunch break anyway. Maybe a quick romp first, but you're still going over to detention afterward."

"How rude to burst into my home without a warrant and try to put hardware on me."

My finger slid into the lace of her bra. "Do you think you should be punished, Officer Greene?"

Her body writhed like a Mojave sidewinder, desperate for more contact. "Punished, yes."

"Let's get you cooled off first. It's *so* hot in here."

"Scorching. Too many clothes…" Her hips raised in a vain attempt to make contact.

"We can't risk wrinkling this fine Metro PD cheap-ass shirt, now can we?"

"No," she moaned. Ava loved kink, and I was happy to oblige. It was certainly more pleasurable than most of my arrests.

One button at a time, as slowly as I could manage, the uniform shirt fell open. "Well, well, Officer Greene. Look at this! I'm pretty sure this black lace contraption isn't department issue. Is it even bulletproof?"

"Hurry, please!" She lacked patience, an unfortunate breach of training.

"You seem sort of agitated – hot, even. I think a little punishment for your earlier rudeness is in order. Then, we'll need to cool you down before we can proceed, Officer."

"Yes, so, so hot! These pants are stifling."

"Are you asking for a bare bottom spanking, Officer? Positively scandalous." With a hard tug, the government-issue cheap wool pants landed on my clean-but-old-as-fuck shag carpeting.

And before we get all up in arms, I knew this girl and she loved a good bit of role-play. I can't even count how many times she was tied to my bed begging for shit she'd read about in those all-the-rage erotica books.

"I don't know, Officer Greene, maybe I'll just turn myself in. The infamous *team* will find you here, like this, with those huge heaving tits out and wearing only whatever this thinner-than-dental-floss lace ribbon thing you've got barely covering that needy, tight place of yours. The felony charge might be worth it."

"Please don't, Mr. Criminal. I've been so very naughty. I think I need a good spanking to set me on the straight and narrow again."

She wasn't the only one mercilessly sweltering in my trailer that day. The strain on my button-fly was unbearable, but it wasn't every day I had a gorgeous, mostly naked cop bound in her own handcuffs on my couch. It was every few days.

"Over you go, like a good girl." She stared at me, desperate to play, but unable to move with her wrists trussed up behind her like a Thanksgiving turkey.

"Roll me over, then," she panted.

"Nah, I have some errands to run. Use some of that PT training those fine Clark County taxpayers forked out for."

The air conditioning in my place was far from great, so I knew the situation would need ice. "Hey Ava, you're lucky I'm out of Rocket Pops today. Remember the last time you needed cooling down?"

She didn't answer, but with a thud she'd managed to flop herself from the couch to the floor.

I glanced over, because I wasn't completely heartless. She was fine. "Aw, damn! Your pretty blue police-person shirt is getting all wrinkled."

"Fuck you, MacKenzie." She was getting more hot and bothered than a Baptist on Fremont Street.

The overly starched uniform top was tangled in a wad around her incapacitated wrists. "No worries, you won't need it. We might need that baton, though. Should I spank you with your own weapon, Officer Greene, or maybe use that thick, wooden rod somewhere else?"

"Not the baton. I had to use it on Bobby the Blob yesterday."

I never could tolerate mess. "And you didn't sanitize it?" I asked, pulling open the freezer door set atop the circa 1950s fridge. "That is positively disgusting, Officer Greene."

She flopped around the carpet again and attempted to get into position. It didn't matter.

"Ah, here. This'll cool your bottom down lickety-split."

"Will you lick it?" she asked from the muffle of my thick carpeting.

"Maybe after I split it."

I walked toward Ava with the tray of ice. "Now let's get you punished so we can get you chilled."

"Do you not have an ice maker, Thug?"

"Aren't we fancy?" I shook my head. "And let's be real – we both know the ice is going to be punishment, too."

Her weight was nothing for my massive frame, even back then. Flipping her face down on the couch was easy, even with the cuffs. "I think we'll leave these shoes on, sort of combat-boot sexy, I think." I tugged at the about-to-tear string of lace covering her wriggling backside. "And this I think will stay, too. We must protect your modesty, Officer Greene."

My hardness pressed against her, teasing but not giving her any friction. She wriggled underneath me, desperate for contact.

"Five or ten?" The palm of my hand cupped her perfectly plump right ass cheek.

"Five."

"Twelve it is. Count perfectly or we'll start over."

By the third playful smack on her skin, Ava had lost all sense of decorum. By five, her imploring wails could probably be heard over the clang of the penny slot machines over at Walgreens. And I shit you not, we did and do have slot machines at Walgreens in Vegas. Hell, they probably even have them at church.

By the time her ample flesh flushed to the perfect shade of pink, I knew she was ready for ice. And yes, there's a perfect shade for each occasion. That day, since she was on a lunch break, Red Rock Red was too much. Besides, the wool-blend trousers would have to eventually go back on. Ava got off the hook that day with a pink the color of the low-water line around Lake Mead.

"Shit, that was hot, you little police-vixen. Most of my ice melted during that spanking."

Her ass wiggled at me, as if tempting me to start the count over. "No time, Greene. Let's get you cooled down."

I lifted her up and flipped her on her backside. I'd need access to her divine *top*side to fully make use of the remains of my ice.

"One side toasty, the other side," I let the ice hit the very tip of her nipple. "The other side frosty."

For a split second, ice is pure pleasure in the Vegas heat. After that, no matter where you are, it's exquisite torture.

Ava craved contact as much as she instinctively fought the bite of the cold on her skin. Her back arched as she moaned for relief.

When she couldn't take another second, I switched to the other side. The warmth of my tongue skimmed her ravished nipples as I let the ice slide lower. She shimmied as it rested in her navel.

"Does that hungry clit need chilling down, Officer Greene? Can't have you overheating."

"No," she pouted and tried to rotate out of my inescapable grasp. "Something warmer."

My tongue skated down her chest toward the melting pool of ice. "You're so wet, Ava."

"Hurry up, Mack. My lunch break is almost over." Poor Ava, so agitated with the pulsing in her combusting nether regions that she broke all role-play protocol.

"*My* midday meal has just begun."

By the time my not-in-a-hurry-in-the-slightest tongue hit her vibrating clit, she was gone. Her orgasmic body shook so hard that I'm pretty sure the tourists from Cali thought San Andreas had found them way out here.

Chapter Three

HAROLD SHOVED UP MY NOSE

"Yeah, that was fun." Ava looked instinctively toward the very same 50s sitcom style freezer I had back then. "You have any ice ready for a repeat session?"

I pulled my perfect daughter close. "Not this time. Not ever, actually. Life has changed for me."

"Yeah, I heard you were shacking up with the social worker, Hank's wife. The one who killed him."

"Killed? Ridiculous." Inside, fury raged. But outside, in front of Ava, I kept it icy-cool. "But yeah, Tara and I are a thing."

She nodded. "Speaking of a thing... Deputy Chief Lane is waiting outside."

"Waiting for?"

"For me to cuff you."

"So you always were a traitor."

"I'm here to help you, Mack."

"Were you around to help me the night Grace's egg donor slit her wrists in the bathtub? Or the countless times they tried to take my daughter from me? Where was Ava, my pal on the force, then?"

She didn't answer.

"Exactly."

"Listen, none of this was my idea. And honestly, I didn't expect you to just come quietly." She shot me a flirty grin despite herself. "You never did. But then again, I didn't expect your little princess to be here for this arrest."

She nervously looked at Grace, who was mercilessly slamming Harold into the side of my curly head.

"This arrest? Ava, you don't want to do this."

"No, I don't. But the Chief needs us. And we need him." She glanced at her phone. "Shit. He's getting impatient. Mack, listen, this isn't what you think."

"It's not you being rolled on to come in here and take me out in one piece?"

"It *is* that. But what he's offering all of us is worth one more hustle."

———

"Lawyer." That was the only word I had for the shady-as-fuck Metro PD.

Deputy Chief Lane sat across my kitchen table from me. "Yeah, we're not that kind of department, MacKenzie."

"Don't I know it." I nodded toward my hands, cuffed behind my back as I sat trussed to my hand-me-down dining chair like a rotisserie chicken. "Is this really necessary? You're freakin' my kid out."

But Grace wasn't at all "freaked out." She was, however, tired, missing mommy, and hungry. And if this pair of Keystone cops thought I was dangerous, they'd never tangled with my hangry toddler.

"Yeah, uh, this is ridiculous, Greene. Uncuff this man before I fire your ass."

Ava was furious. "But you told me to—" I shook my head at her. I knew damn well he'd ordered her to subdue me. I'd never escape the reputation I'd built in Vegas.

As she removed the restraints, Chief Lane pointed to my now-unloaded gun on the table between us. "How'd you like to carry that legally?"

"That's not my gun. I've never seen it before. I'm pretty sure you planted it."

"Cut the bullshit, MacKenzie. I don't have time for it. Besides, that little blue-eyed gangster you brought into the world with the crazy stripper is hungry. And then there's your other crazy ex…"

"Don't talk about Dawn."

"*That* one is batshit crazy. Didn't she try to burn your kid at the stake?"

"Something like that." My psychotic ex had actually tried to sacrifice Grace Old Testament style in some Abraham and Isaac re-creation out in the canyon.

Chief Lane glanced at his phone, as if he had all day. "She's not that securely locked up, by the way. I can help you with that. But first, here's my offer. No faking this time – I need to fully deputize you. It's imperative that all of it hold up in court."

"How are you going to arrange that?" I was getting impatient. Even this crooked-ass operation had to have some standards about who they let carry bronze stars around.

"Well, we're going to clear your record. A full expunge – like it never happened."

"Manslaughter – just never happened?"

"It's all hazy to me. New evidence clears you, whatever. Think about it. I mean if I had a new family and a promising career…"

"And the cost of this amnesia?" I knew the price would

be high. But the payoff…my heart jumped at the possibility. Not for me, but for Grace and Tara. To not have "convicted felon" hanging over their futures – it was beyond tempting.

"The cost is forty-eight hours of your time. We've already cleared it with your famous MMA fighter boss, actually. I made him an offer he couldn't refuse."

"And I'm going to do what in those two days?" Grace climbed into my lap and shoved her mass of wild curls into my chest. It was like she knew we were about to be tested. That kid had wicked good intuition.

"The Juric crime family – I need some information from them."

I *actually* laughed out loud.

"If you could just listen to—"

"No, Chief. No fuckin' way. Anything having to do with the J-word isn't coming anywhere near me. Those guys are lethal."

I was born in Vegas and knew better – I stayed far from that type of organized crime. Especially the Jurics.

"I get it. But it's not them I need. A guy who works for them has information that is imperative to my investigation. You need to talk to, and arrest, their hitman."

"Sounds like a video game mission."

"Yeah, well, to me this is no game. It's personal."

"Why me?"

"The hitman is someone you know. I was told that you were close back during your days locked up together at Ely."

"I'm not close to people, Chief. Sorry."

"As close as anyone can be to Krsto the Carver, then."

Krsto the Carver. Holy fuck. "I haven't seen him in years. Has he bought a vowel yet?"

"Maybe you can joke with him about his moniker

while you get the information I need and slap cuffs on him. My sources tell me you had a connection with him?"

"I did, yeah. He's the one who taught me to box during those endless hours in the state pen. But me? Arrest him? That guy isn't going to get pinched without a brawl."

"Your job is to peacefully arrest him. The last couple of attempts have… Well, they haven't gone as well as I'd hoped. But we've located him again, so the clock is ticking."

"And you're asking me to turn on him?" I knew I couldn't do that, not even for the Chief's dangling offer of redemption.

"Look, I'm not asking that. My beef isn't with Krsto or his bosses. The arrest, and removing him from the area, is for his protection. The guys I need info on will see him as a snitch whether he gives us evidence or not."

"And if I don't? If I just say no and head over to the gym to do my real job?"

He let out a long sigh. His fingers drummed on a folder in front of us. "As a father, I'm sure you prefer to guide with positive reinforcement rather than negative feedback to get the behavior you want. Correct?"

"Grace rarely gives me the behavior I want." She was trying to shove Harold up my nose at that very moment.

"Let's just say the reward I'm offering is unprecedented. And believe what you will about this department, much of it true, but I *am* one of the good ones. But for this, I'll get as muddy as I need to. I'm fully prepared to arrest you for the murder of Detective Hank Larsen."

"I thought he was missing? Ran off to Mexico or something?" Tara's ex-husband had been as evil as they'd come, and we'd dealt with him accordingly. I knew for a fact that there was no bloated, hairy body left to surface anywhere, ever.

"You do this, MacKenzie, or I swear to God there will be an identifiable corpse ripe with all of the latest DNA scientific shit to put you and your lady away for good."

I didn't flinch, not for a second.

"Tell him, Darren!" Ava had been silent as long as her nature allowed. Now she was behind him, her hands intimately perched on his shoulders.

"Enough, Officer Greene." He brushed her hands away and gestured for her to sit.

"Mack, it's his daughter. They've got her. You of all people should understand that! I think it's the same crew that tried to take Grace when she was a newborn."

"If that's true, she's probably already in Russia."

His steely gray eyes met mine. A mist of sweat formed on his balding head. "She's still in the country. But she wasn't exactly abducted – she fell in love with the wrong guy."

"She's seventeen, Mack." Ava was desperate to convince me.

Chief Lane leaned in toward me. "I'm asking you as a father. Information, the guy's name, where they're running their racket out of. That's all I need."

"You've got the paperwork? Some proof you'll hold up your end if I do this?"

He slid a document across the table. It was legit.

I pulled Grace closer. One more sacrifice would be worth a chance at redemption.

"I need to take my kid back to the hotel and tell Tara what's up."

He pulled the paper, my chance at freedom, at a future without the cloud of the conviction, away from me.

"No, you can't tell her. I can't risk them getting wind that we're coming. The deal is off if you utter one syllable to anyone. We're about to wire you up to make sure those hairy lips don't get loose. Make something up, but if you mention any of this I'll make life *very* unpleasant for you, MacKenzie."

I knew it wasn't going to be easy. Tara could smell a lie as if it were a tuna sandwich left all day in a hot car.

———

The gleaming floors of the Red Rock Resort were night and day from the 70s shag carpet of my Sam's Town trailer.

It took two minutes for Oliver and his entourage to spot me from his usual perch in the opulent lobby bar. "Hey, Gangsta, find some summer shoes!"

He was clearly several Tito's and Tonics in. Normally, as his trainer for the biggest comeback of his life, I'd have lost my shit about it. But that day, I was relieved he was too tipsy to see through my bullshit.

"Yeah, uh, well, I think I only own like three pairs of shoes." My battered black boots certainly didn't fit in with the upscale surroundings.

"After this fight you'll be able to afford a fucking shoe factory. Except, of course, I was told earlier that my main trainer is abandoning me."

I was highly conscious of the listening device wrapped around my chest. "I'm really sorry about that, Oliver. This thing came up out of the blue." I had no idea what they'd told him.

"Hey, if it'll get you out of the po-lice crosshairs, it's all good. Besides, they're gonna hook me up with some immigration favors as thanks for doing without you for a couple of days."

"Ah, that's cool then." I had no idea what to say.

Grace smacked me with Harold and tugged at my shirt. *Saved by the kid.*

"Mini gangsta girl is not having it!" Oliver howled. "She's gonna be a badass."

"True that." I lifted her up and with a quick wave, we escaped toward the elevators.

———

"Oh good, you found Harold."

Tara was standing in the luxurious kitchenette. My boss, Oliver, put his whole crew and their families up in style when we traveled. The suite at Red Rock was beyond anything I'd ever imagined a poor white trash boy from the wrong side of the city staying at.

"Yeah, she's been pummeling me with him ever since."

. "She's definitely a better boxer than you, Shawn." She was the love of my life and the only one allowed to call me by my given name.

"True that."

Her head cocked to one side, as if waiting for me to make some statement. I had no idea what the fuck I was going to tell her. I only knew it couldn't be the truth.

She reached for Grace and snuggled her close. "So Oliver's nanny said she could take care of Grace." Her eyes searched my face, as if we shared some tantalizing secret.

"Why?"

"He said you asked for a couple of days off?"

We all knew that was something I would never do – take time off before a fight.

"Yeah, that. I have some shit to take care of back, uh, just some stuff." It was a horrible attempt at being skillfully evasive.

"Oh." She let the wiggling Grace down and walked to the floor-to-ceiling window. "The canyon is so gorgeous this time of day. San Francisco is great but nothing compares to desert sunsets."

She was hurt. "Tara, I can explain."

But I couldn't. The wrong words from me and my deal would be off the table. And worse – I knew from the look in the Chief's eyes, he'd make good on his threats as well as promises. Despite his stone-cold coolness on the outside, inside he was a desperate father. I understood that all too well.

I stepped behind her and wrapped my arms around her waist. She'd been through so much that summer, and all of it my fault. "I need you to trust me. Don't ask, don't talk. Just take care of Grace and stay low."

"How silly I was. For a split second I thought you were taking me on an engagement trip or something."

"I will, I promise. After the fight, after this thing I've got to do."

Chapter Four

EVERY REPULSIVE TROLL THAT HAS EVER JACKED OFF

I was an hour late to meet Ava back at Sam's Town.

I didn't care. Being buried in Tara until she fell asleep was worth it.

"What time's the flight? Sorry I'm late."

Ava was in some nondescript sedan with a giant designer coffee hovering at her overly-glittered lips. Unlike earlier, she looked nothing like a cop. As she glanced over at me, her trademark long wavy chestnut lock of hair drifted over her face.

"We're driving."

"What? To fucking New York? You said Krsto was working for Juric, right?"

"He's in Tacoma, actually. And I can't risk them seeing us coming in on an airline manifest and that asswipe Sheriff has the department's jet out in Pahrump."

"What the actual fuck?" Our nearest sin-loving neighbor out in Nye County was an hour drive away, max. Prostitution was legal there, but a crew of high-level Clark County cops showing up in a jet was a new level of brazen gluttony.

Ava rolled her eyes at the thought. "Yeah, apparently there were too many of them headed to their *meeting* for the choppers. It was all over the news this afternoon."

"Lots of good police conferencing going on at the Chicken Ranch, I'm sure."

She motioned for me to buckle up. "Yep, so it's road trip city for us tonight. Tacoma or bust."

"Shit, that'll take…"

"Seventeen hours plus change."

———

"What's in this for you?"

Ava's eyes flashed in the rearview mirror. She said nothing. We were only a few hours into our long drive.

"C'mon, Aves, what you gettin'? A promotion? A little extra cut of the take?"

"You know I never wanted to do that, Mack. I had no choice – if you're not taking like everyone else, you're an outsider. And being an outsider in that department is dangerous."

"Don't I know it."

"Well, Chief Lane is trying to change all that. He's a good guy." She pointed to my torso, where the listening device was snaked across the giant inked wings on my chest.

I aimed my middle finger at it. "Oh yeah, your buddy the benevolent *Darren*. Sure he is." I cracked open my third Red Bull. "The same straight and narrow pillar of law enforcement who plans to plant evidence against me and destroy my family. That upstanding citizen?" I lifted my shirt and spoke right into the microphone. "Right, asshole?"

"He's not listening now. Estelle was dragging him to some church function tonight."

"Estelle?" I raised an eyebrow.

"Wife. It's complicated. But despite that, he *is* a good man, Mack. It's just he's beyond desperate. And there's *nothing* in it for me, probably not even him. But I've met Sarah, and they've got her wrapped up hard in this prostitution ring."

"That's his kid?"

She nodded. "Yeah, they tried to hide her, but he got wind that they were working the Tacoma docks. And then when he found out Krsto was doing a job in Tacoma, he saw an opportunity. That's when he approached me about you."

"Ah," I said. "So that's the tie in with Krsto. You do know that entire area is Panda territory, right?"

"Yeah," she nodded. "Let's hope we're in and out before the Tongans get wind of any of it."

Ava was nervous. I couldn't blame her – that organization was lethal if you crossed them wrong. And, unfortunately, almost any crossing of Panda and his crew of deadly Polynesians was wrong.

"Well, Ava, I need to take a shower. You don't go hang with some high-level mafia hitman emitting sweaty road trip fumes." My half-naked body was clearly causing her some agitation.

She peered around the corners of the seedy motel room, as if some fairy would bless me with clean-dust. "I've already told you no. The wire can't get wet."

"So you guys strap this shit on to people and expect them to keep it dry?"

"No, not usually. This one was surplus. This endeavor isn't exactly the Sheriff's priority."

"Nah, it can't compete with jetting off to cat houses."

"It's better if we keep this under the radar. That deal that you got is best kept quiet."

"Okay, then the ghetto-ass wire is coming off. So is everything else."

"S-stop! Wait, let me call Darren."

I dropped the next layer of clothing. "You've been calling him all fucking day. Clearly he's not nearly as interested as you are."

"Story of my life," she muttered. "Can't you just do like a sponge bath for now?"

The rest of my dirty laundry dropped and I stood naked in front of her. "Do you have a sponge that big?"

She made a lame attempt at diverting her eyes. "Ugh, you can't, uh... This is a professional operation, Mr. MacKenzie, please put something on." She pointed to the wire, worried about what the absent Chief Lane would suppose. As for me, I didn't give two fucks what he supposed.

"Whatever, you've seen it all before. This time it's just touchless, like those classy car washes. Now, how do I yank this tape off without removing a layer of skin?"

"Let's wait until he calls me back. I'm sure he's—"

"He's married. And you're clearly way down his priority list." With a yank, I tossed their stupid K-Mart quality monitoring device to the floor and headed to the shower.

———

When I came out soaking wet, she was sitting cross-legged on the motel bed. "Bedspread!" I pointed.

"Huh?" She glanced down at the decades-old cloth she was perched on.

"Your body is touching the same unwashed, bacteria-laden bedspread that every repulsive troll has ever jacked off on. That thing is straight from a 1970s Holiday Inn. Get off of it before I dip you in bleach." I was an epic-level neat freak.

She shrugged. "Fine. It's not like we're sleeping here anyway. And I didn't have much of a choice of establishments. We needed a cash only place and two rooms would have looked weird."

"Indeed." I reached for my clothes, having zero modesty as usual, as I let the tiny towel drop. "Coffee. Do you think you could procure us some?" I knew it'd be another sleepless night, and I'd driven most of the way there.

"Oh, coffee. Yeah, good idea. There's one of those machines over on the counter."

I stared at her, wondering how she'd survived the past twenty-nine years on the planet without contracting a flesh-eating illness. "I thought you quit smokin' crack, Ava? Never use those."

"Fine! I'll go get some. But I'm not supposed to leave you alone."

"In case I what? Disappear? If I wanted to be gone, I would have been gone. Now go get us some coffee, pretty please, Officer Greene." My tattooed fingers formed into the prayer gesture. I was willing to humble myself for some good brew.

She glanced at the wire on the floor. "He'll hear if you do anything."

"Sure he will."

"There's a gas station next door. Do you want anything to eat?"

"Ava Greene, do you *eat* at gas stations?" I shuddered at the thought.

She shrugged. "Well, not 7-Eleven nachos or anything. You know the ones with the plastic cheese? Yeah, I gave those up. Well, mostly."

I cringed at the thought of allowing a cheese-colored liquid synthetic to enter the sanctity of my body. "Just no."

"I confess I do sometimes roll through the Terrible Herbst's on Hacienda after a long shift for those yummy beef hoagies, though."

"And the fact that the place is literally named 'Terrible' doesn't clue you in as to the quality of their cuisine?"

"I work long hours, Mack. Maybe you could send me over your personal chef or something."

"I'll do better than that. The second we get back, you're going on an eating plan. But for now, we need coffee ASAP." I was a caffeine addict, and the tiny silver cans of stimulant I'd been pounding were wearing off. "And Ava, not from a fucking gas station. Go get the good stuff."

"Good stuff? Where?"

"Hello, we're not that far from the holy grail of java. Figure it out."

Sending her off in the middle of the afternoon straight into snarly I-5 traffic was a sure way to get some privacy. Seattle would keep Ava busy for hours, but at the expense of my energy fix.

Chapter Five

THE TACOMA AROMA

Ava was angrier than a vegan at the Heart Attack Grill when she finally returned from her caffeine quest.

"Ah, cool. I hope it's still hot." I barely even glanced up from my phone as I reached toward the cardboard cupholder.

I was lucky Ava didn't throw the paper cups of coffee in my face. "Traffic was a nightmare, and do you have any earthly idea how far from here downtown Seattle is, Mack?"

"Kind of tepid, but thanks for getting this." I sipped at one of the tall cups of what was now iced coffee.

She was about to explode. "You sent me over an hour in *each* direction."

I threw my hands in the air. "I said go get Starbucks. No big deal."

"The address you put in my GPS sent me to 1912 Pike Place, as in Pike Place Market! To the *original* Starbucks."

With a laugh, I gulped down my cold coffee. "You're so

gullible. Anyway, while you were out playing tourist, I was here getting some actual work done."

"You're an ass. And have you smelled it out there? It positively reeks. I guess it was worth driving to Seattle just to avoid that stench."

"It's paper and humidity, I think." I had a ridiculously sensitive sense of smell.

"No, it's sewage," she argued. She pulled out her phone. "Holy shit, Wiki says it's the Tacoma Aroma. You're right – paper and tidewater stagnation."

"See? Told you so."

But her focus wasn't on Tacoma lore. Her eyes were locked on my bare chest, and not in her usual thirsty girl kind of way. "Where's the wire?"

"Ava, Ava, Ava." I said. "We both know that wasn't real."

"What? Are you deranged?"

"Where was the white van listening?"

"White van? MacKenzie, I don't have time for this. Put the wire back on."

"I flushed it."

She bolted toward the bathroom, her hands reaching into the foul abyss that was the toilet. "It was real, Einstein. That U-Haul truck down the block has been following us since we left Vegas."

"I knew that," I lied.

"Holy shit, it's still in here. Let's hope the water didn't kill it."

I hoped the water *did* kill it. There was zero chance I was going to let my old prison sparring mate implicate himself on audio. "Do you think the U-Haul guys could go get us some hot coffee?"

The wet listening device, crawling with toilet water

dwelling microscopic monsters, struck me square in the side of my giant head.

———

"I told Krsto I was in town for some Saints & Sinners shit. They have dealings here in Tacoma. He's going to meet us at a dive bar down on the docks."

"Us?"

I nodded. "I can't wear this wire, Ava. That's the first thing he's going to check."

She'd managed to get some sort of sign of life out of the now sanitized device. "I can't. He'll know I'm a cop in seconds."

"You are the most un-cop looking cop I've ever seen. So get ready to slut it up, Buttercup. I told him I was bringing my side chick."

"Classy."

"Always. Listen, if you insist on wearing this James Bond shit make sure it's wadded up in your bra. If I offer you up to Krsto, I'll just tell him you have new implants and can't take it off."

"That's not happening!"

Caffeine, little sleep, and a pissed off cop - it was the perfect time to tease her even further. "That's what happens undercover. If you don't actually let yourself get passed around, we could all die. Haven't you ever watched *Sons of Anarchy*?"

"Fuck you, Mack." She stormed off toward her boys in the listening truck, and I took the opportunity to make one more phone call while the insidious wire was out of the room.

———

He didn't look much different. I guess neither did I.

"Hey, K. How ya been?" I slapped him on the back, hard enough to prove I was the same bold motherfucker I always was.

"Still lethal as fuck. How's life treating you, Bro?" His dark eyes met mine.

"Most definitely it's on the rise. There's that bit I told you about earlier, but other than that, life is smooth." Ava's eyes met mine – she trusted me about as much as a gaming commissioner trusted a casino.

A humongous bartender slammed down a bowl of stale nuts on the sticky bar in front of the three of us. "Whatcha want?" A warm welcome it was not.

Ava, breaking all thug protocol, piped up. I guess she was used to ladies first. "A chardonnay, please. Kendall Jackson, nine ounces."

All three of us stared at her. "The wine here is in a can, babycakes," the bartender finally said.

"Oh, um, that sounds super hipster. Like craft beer or something?"

I was pretty sure at the very least no one suspected that she was a hardened Vegas cop. I also knew she wasn't acting - Ava was a complex gal.

The bartender leaned in toward her heaving cleavage. "This is Tacoma, not fucking Seattle, honey. And canned wine is *always* shit."

"Oh, cool, thanks for the heads up. Then I'll have a double shot of Jack, neat."

He cocked his head to the side with a new admiration for Ava. "I'm Bones, by the way. You give me a whistle if you need anything, pretty lady."

"Red Bull, two of them," I said, interrupting the flirt-fest.

His reptilian head pivoted toward me. "What kind of a man doesn't drink?" Bones asked.

Krsto stood up and got inches from the bartender's face. "The last time I saw this man drink, he shoved a plastic prison spork into a motherfucker's eye."

I nodded. "Yeah, tequila made me crazy. But that guy was looking at me wrong, to be fair." I reached for the peanuts. "Hey, are these organic?"

Bones didn't fuck with me after that.

———

Krsto was on his third beer when he finally decided to cut through the bullshit. "Listen, Mack, I'm going to assume that whatever I say is going straight into that wire taped to your chest."

I lifted my shirt, much to a few pool playing ladies' delight. "Nope."

"Obviously it's lower, probably wrapped around your sweaty balls, but I've seen enough of your naked ass when we shared a cell to last a lifetime. The skinny is I don't know shit about those particular Russians you asked me about on the phone. The Jurics don't get involved in that sort of low hangin' fruit. People's kids are off limits."

"Oh," Ava said, suddenly very interested in our conversation. "You *talked* on the *phone*? Was that this afternoon? Because I was under the impression you'd only exchanged a quick message to set up this reunion."

I knew damn well that stupid listening device in her heavily padded push-up bra wouldn't record a thing. Still, she leaned in closer to Krsto as if she had me trapped.

He tore at the label of his bottle of Bud. "I can't recall."

Her eyes met mine. She knew I was up to something. She should've known that I was *always* up to something.

And she should have *also* known that I would never betray an associate. But still, I did have sympathy for the Chief's position. And to be honest, I was still hoping to get my own ass out of hot water in the process.

I looked to the back of the room. Two men in suits stood out like a down parka in Vegas. They'd been watching Krsto the entire time, and he knew it. Lane had been right – he wasn't safe talking to us. Even worse, I'd gotten none of the information I needed to seal my deal.

"So interestingly enough, my buddy said he heard you were doing police shit out here."

I wasn't surprised, but Ava was. She spit a mouthful of her Jack Daniels all over the bar. News travels lightning fast in the sordid world of cops and crooks, and one of the surveillance guys Lane trusted to travel with us probably ratted to the local crime network.

"So it seems there's some confusion, Mack. But I know you aren't really a cop," he said with a chuckle. "Mack MacKenzie would never do that shit. You're helping them though, right?"

Ava was losing her shit. I was completely deviating from the script they'd given me.

"Sorry, K. I didn't have a choice. We really need that info."

"I don't know shit about that sex trafficking thing. Tacoma ain't my territory – you know that. And even if I did, there's no way I could talk about the Russians without getting my own neck slit."

"So we move to plan B. I can arrest you or let you walk out of here and those suits are going to *assume* you *did* give me the information I need."

He emptied his beer and shot a side glance at the men. "It'll go down like we talked about?"

I nodded. "Yep, Bro. And I'll owe you one."

Leaning in close, he said in my ear, "I hope you fuck them up hard."

I reached into the back of my jeans and pulled out the cuffs I'd been entrusted with. "I think I need a set of these as a souvenir of this little adventure," I said to Ava, who was not amused.

"Alright, my friend, Tacoma PD is waiting outside. I'm pretty sure they even saved you a donut."

With a deep breath, he stood up and put his hands behind his back. "What a fucked up universe it is when Mack fucking MacKenzie is cuffing motherfuckers!"

I had to admit, it was most definitely fucked up.

———

A local squad car drove away with Krsto safely in its grasp. What Ava *didn't* know was that as soon as it evaded the gangsters following it, Krsto would walk free. In our brief clandestine phone call earlier that afternoon, he'd told me that most of the Tacoma Police Department was on Juric family payroll.

Ava looked defeated.

"What now?" She sat on the stool next to me with an actual wineglass in her hands. Apparently, Bones could produce fine fruit of the grape if he liked you enough. And he seemed to be drooling over Ava.

"We go home." I missed my kid like crazy and avoiding Tara's texts was killing me.

"Not without Sarah. We're finding her, Mack."

I drained the last of my third energy drink. "That wasn't the deal."

"The deal was you get info on who has her. You didn't do jack shit besides betray us!"

"I *did* try. He wasn't going to offer anyone up even if he knew, which he didn't."

"Those guys watching us, the ones that followed him out? Clearly they're connected!"

I shook my head. "I doubt it. I think they're part of Juric's crew making sure their hitman doesn't get too cozy with the cops, nothing more."

"So are you two together?" Bones was standing in front of us refilling Ava's already full glass. "Because I've got a mattress upstairs if not."

"What the fuck?" Ava was offended, but Bones wasn't on my agenda to tangle with. I poked her in the thigh as a reminder of her undercover status.

He seemed stung by her less than positive reaction to his crude request to fornicate.

Bones regrouped and tried again. "Oh, I meant, we could have some frozen pizzas maybe and watch the fight?"

"That sounds, um, nice." She faked her best smile. "But I'm committed to this one."

He looked to me. "Yeah, baby in the oven and all. Otherwise, you know, we could be more cordial."

I knew damn well that Bones' invitation wasn't hinged on whether or not she was single. It also wasn't an offer we could safely refuse. I was hoping Bones would have the courtesy to pass on a knocked-up chick. The guy was the size of a tank, and I really didn't want to tangle with him if I could avoid it diplomatically.

Ava leaned in, wrapping herself around me like an octopus. "Yeah, and the doc said no messing around." Her hand went to her flat belly.

Bones nodded and pointed to her glass. "Go easy on the vino, then. More than a bottle is bad for a kid, I think."

He moved down the bar as Ava breathed a sigh of relief. "That was close!" she said, her head falling to my chest.

And then, at that very moment, I saw her.

As if my night couldn't have gotten any worse, Tara was staring daggers at us from across the crowded bar.

Chapter Six

FORNICATING AT THE PANDA EXPRESS

"Tara, I can explain."

I'd followed her into the bathroom after extracting Ava's tipsy hands from the crevices of my body.

"Shut the eff up, Shawn." Before I could say a word, her lips slammed into mine with a fury I'd never known from her.

She was everything I'd ever wanted, but never even knew existed. My fingers wrapped through her hair as my tongue devoured her. "I need you now," she panted.

"Not here, it's filthy. Let's get out of here and—"

"Now. Here. Fuck me like an animal, MacKenzie."

Holy shit, Tara said the mother of all swear words.

I was instantly hard as hell, germs or no germs. In seconds I had the formidable barrier that was her skinny jeans off of her. She moaned as our lips crashed into each other. Pulling her hair even harder, I bit at her lower lip. This wasn't the time for softness. She wanted primal and I intended to deliver.

I could hear activity in the ladies' room behind us, but

neither of us cared. At that moment of pure passion, she was my entire universe and nothing else mattered.

My jeans dropped to my ankles as her desperate fingers wrapped around my throbbing cock. I was sure I'd explode in her skilled hand if I wasn't inside her soon. "Get these off," I grunted, tugging at the cotton that was in my way.

She glanced down momentarily at her choice of under-garment for the day. "Crap, I should have worn those fancy ones."

"No one cares." My teeth sank into the side of her luscious neck as the briefs labeled "Tuesday" fell to the ground. It was Friday, for the record.

Her now free legs climbed up me like a monkey scaling a tree. For a split second I worried the rattling metal door would burst open, but then I realized it wouldn't matter. I was too far gone with burning fury for her. I would have fucked her on the bathroom sink with the entire bar watching at that moment.

"Harder," she begged as I slammed into her.

The stall shook as the bathroom chatter went silent. Either we were in the vortex of our own combustion, or they were listening. We didn't care. I was pretty sure they could hear the normally quiet Tara moaning all the way back home in Sam's Town that night.

Her legs shook as they wrapped around my waist. "That's so deep," she howled as she pulsed around me. Her entire core squeezed mercilessly as I thrust into her like a man possessed. I *was* possessed – possessed by her.

Balancing her against the wall, I managed to get a thumb to her clit. One slow, delicious circle and she was shivering, begging. "I'm going to come," she panted.

Those four words were all I needed to explode deep inside her in perfect orgasmic ecstasy.

Afterward, I held her close to me, both of us panting as we recovered from the powerful climax.

"Angry sex with you is hot as hell," I whispered into her ear. We were out of breath, our bodies still joined as one. But I felt her stiffen.

She pulled away from me. "Maybe it was break-up sex, Shawn."

My knees buckled. "Please don't ever say that, Tara. Losing you would shatter me. I'd never survive it."

"You would."

"I love *you*. This thing with Ava isn't what it looks like."

"I don't want to hear it."

"I tried to call this afternoon, but you didn't answer. It wasn't something I could text, so—"

"Shawn, I *really* don't need you to explain. You should know Becky sees *everything*."

Becky had been my next-door neighbor at the trailer park. She was a master level snoop and gossip. "Wait, Becky?"

She nodded. "Yes. In her infinite wisdom, she wrote on my Facebook wall that you were seen canoodling with 'that cop whore Ava Greene' again."

"Fuck." I leaned back against the metal stall. "Wait, Becky said *canoodling*?"

"No, she used a string of expletives that my grandmother certainly enjoyed."

"Damn. Poor Granny Agatha."

"It might have been nice for Becky to deliver her TMZ blast via a private message, but I already knew you were lying to me."

"I *had* to."

"I know, Shawn. The *last* thing that went through my mind was that you were screwing around. So I did some snooping."

"Tenacious as always." I took a deep breath, relieved that our bond had withstood yet another test. "But you shouldn't have come."

"*Someone* has to save your behind." I grinned at the term "behind." Tara almost never swore, and the contrast with her rare dirty talk minutes earlier was cute as hell.

"I've got this worked out. Please, go back to Grace. I'll get one of the Saints & Sinners guys to take you home while I finish up here."

"No, Shawn, we're doing this together. After her public blast, I went to see Becky. She eventually mentioned that she'd seen a hot cop in a fancy uniform hovering outside of your trailer. It didn't take much digging for me to figure out she was talking about Darren Lane."

"Yeah, this is all about his kid."

She nodded. "I know. My dad is friendly with Chief Lane *and* his wife. A little persuasion from dear ol' dad and Darren filled us in on the offer they made you. *And* the threat to both of us."

"I don't spook easily, Tara. But it wouldn't take much for him to have us both locked up for Hank's disappearance." There were too many listening ears around to openly discuss Tara's lecherous ex-husband's demise.

"That's not happening. Dad put the fear of Jesus into him. Or the fear of the wrath of John Drake, I guess."

"So it's over then? Let's get out of here. We didn't get what we needed. Krsto won't talk."

"Not until we do what you came to do."

"Listen, Tara, your trust means the world to me. But you can't be here. It's dangerous. This is Panda's territory, and I'm sure as fuck we're no longer under the radar. None of us will get out of here alive if we don't hustle."

"Yeah, messing with the Polynesians is a *bad* idea. You

have no idea how much crap you and Officer Giant Boobs are in right now."

"Wait, how do you know about Tacoma shit?"

She shot me a wink. "*That's* why I came to help. My Uncle Pete is here and might be persuaded to assist us, but I needed to come in person. He'd never talk to the cops, and he's seen you with Ava tonight so you're not high on his list either. And of course, Dad is banned from Washington."

Tara's father, John Drake, the former Clark County police chief, was always dabbling in shady shit. His being banned from an entire state didn't surprise me in the slightest. "So your dear ol' dad sent you here alone? Into this viper's nest of organized crime?" I was furious at my future father-in-law.

"Not alone. But listen, we need to work quickly."

"Huh?"

"I need in your pants again."

It took me seconds to have my junk out for round two, but she shook her head.

"No time for *that*." She reached into her pocket and pulled out a tiny metal disc about the size of a watch battery. "But this needs to go in that magic place where my fingertip presses right at the moment of—"

"You're going to bug me *there*?"

She licked her lips. "Yeah. Uncle Pete won't check *there*, and your friend at the FBI who loaned it to me said it's super sensitive. Just like *that* place."

Her fingers ran down me, searching for the magical spot. "Stop fondling me or I'm going to fuck you again, and we really need to hustle out of here. Panda could show up at any minute."

Panda was the head of the entire Pacific gang of Polynesians. Of Tongan decent, he was a massive presence both physically and in his control of the West Coast. He was well respected among the crime organizations and law enforcement alike, but he notoriously didn't tolerate intrusions on his territory. And that bar, and those docks, were his territory.

She zipped my fly and gestured toward the door. "Actually, Panda is here. And he wants to speak to *you*."

———

Not much scared me, but an audience with Panda wasn't high on my list of desirable experiences. "We have to find a back way out. He'll kill me."

Tara seemed completely oblivious to the danger we were in. "C'mon," she said, tugging at my hand.

But as I turned, I ran into what felt like a brick wall.

"Bones, stop! Leave him alone. That's his fiancée!" Ava was pulling at the massive giant's shirt.

Tara screamed as Bones wrapped his hand around my throat. "One baby mama drinking away her sorrows while you fuck another bitch in the bathroom? I'm gonna kill you!"

He was strong and big as hell, but unfortunately for Bones he was slow. A right hook to his kidneys, a swift thrust of my knee to his balls, and he let go of my throat.

I had it under control and was just about to knock him out when Ava decided to intervene.

"We're cops! You're under arrest." She whipped out her badge as Bones' evil eyes met mine. She had no idea what a huge mistake she'd just made.

"Then you're *all* gonna die!"

He reached for Ava as a booming voice spoke from behind us. "Well isn't that interesting?"

42

Everyone froze as Panda walked toward us. He was not amused.

———

Fuck. We were completely and utterly screwed.

Bones leaned against the wall, terrified of the ominous presence.

Tara, however, pulled away from me and walked right up to the man. I tried to think of how to save her as she got within inches of him.

"Uncle Pete, thanks so much for coming to meet me."

To my utter shock, the man laughed a deep belly laugh and opened his arms to hug her. "Tara, girl. It's no trouble at all. I own this bar, after all. In fact, I own them all throughout these docks."

"Daddy would have come but you know of his troubles here over that whole Strippergate nonsense."

"Such ridiculousness. John was only doing what the governor paid him to do. But please, let's all go into the back room. I have some questions for this man who claims to love you."

A panicked voice interrupted. "Sir, I was simply…" Bones looked at his boss in fear.

"Go on upstairs, Bones. Take the night off."

"Yes, sir." The giant, still holding his aching balls, trudged away from us.

"*Uncle* Pete?" I whispered to Tara as we followed Panda toward the bolted door at the back of the bar.

"Yeah. His given name is Pekelo, but I couldn't say that when I was little. So I just started calling him Uncle Pete."

"I can see the family resemblance – *not*."

"Of course he's not my *biological* uncle. Many of my dad's cronies ended up being uncle figures. I'm guessing the Panda nickname is because he looks like a giant cuddly panda bear."

"Cuddly isn't exactly the first adjective that came to mind."

"Well, he's pretty pissed off at you, but he'll come around."

"I'm guessing he saw Becky's post?"

She nodded. "Yep, and then his guy on the local police force informs him that you're here *with* her. You're both lucky I got here before he did."

"Yeah, how'd you get here so fast?"

"I borrowed the Sheriff's jet."

What the fuck?

"The boss doesn't have all day," an armed guard barked from the back of the bar.

———

Behind the armored door, the place looked like a 20s speakeasy. Jazz music rolled out of speakers from the ceiling. Pool tables and leather sofas surrounded the bar-within-a-bar.

"Why shouldn't I filet this cheating imposter?" He pointed a hefty finger into my face. Panda had a reputation for gutting people he didn't like as if they were fish.

"Stop it, Uncle Pete. I already told you – it's all a misunderstanding. They're undercover."

"So I heard." He turned a deep crimson, which didn't make me feel that my entrails were any safer. "You brought cops into my lair!"

"Cut the drama, Uncle. You know darn well this whole place is crawling with cops in various stages of legality. Besides, *Dad* is a cop."

He exhaled slowly, his face returning to its normal shade. "Technically you're right, I suppose."

"So there was no cheating, and your favorite niece is just fine," Tara reassured him.

Panda reached his mammoth right hand out to me. "Well, then, it's nice to meet you, Mr. MacKenzie."

"Mack," I managed to say.

He gestured for us all to sit. "What is it I can do for you, Mack?"

I had no idea how to handle getting Panda to talk. Luckily, Ava piped up and told him the entire story. True to her obsession with Chief Lane, she poured it on thick.

Panda stroked the goatee on his chin as he listened to her. When she'd finally finished her plea, he leaned back in his seat.

"*I*, of course, would not speak to any of that."

I wasn't in the slightest bit surprised. You don't stay at the top by talking.

"Of course you wouldn't," Tara said, placing her hand on his forearm. "But you mentioned an employee who might be willing to share some observations he'd made?"

Panda nodded. "Yes, a dockworker of ours came to me recently concerned about the trafficking of young women through our territory. *We* never engage in that type of revenue."

"Would he be willing to talk to us?" Ava asked.

"For a price. And because *you*, lovely Ava, have been so very convincing, *I* will pay his price."

Ava smiled wide at Panda, batting her eyelashes as if she had a new crush. I suspected she wasn't acting this time.

"Uncle Pete, to make it so that they can get this to hold up in court, would he be willing to talk to the Deputy

Chief from Las Vegas? We flew in together, and he's respectfully waiting outside."

"The girl you spoke of is his daughter?"

"Yes," Tara said with a nod. "Seventeen."

"Fine," Panda said with a deep exhale.

———

Hours later, we sat around the pool tables in Panda's back room. The dockworker had given Chief Lane everything he needed to start the search for his daughter.

Tara clinked her bottle of Stella against the Chief's tumbler of whiskey. "I can't believe you got a federal judge to grant that wiretap warrant so fast."

Darren grinned at her. "I have my connections, and John helped." He held up the small device that contained the evidence he needed.

"Make sure you wash that, Chief. I got fairly intimate with it, if you know what I mean."

He cringed and let the bug drop to the table. "Noted. And hey, your paperwork has already been filed by the DA back in Vegas."

I felt a wave of relief wash over me. At least one part of my sordid past would no longer haunt me. "So what now?" I asked.

"Now you all go back to Vegas with my gratitude."

"What about you? You've got a name, a rough location now, but Sarah is still out there."

Darren's face fell. "Yes, and it's terrifying. I'll die trying to get her home if I have to."

Ava slid her hand into his, but he pulled back. "Ava, you know how I feel about you. But I can't give you that."

"But you haven't even shared a room with her in years!"

He looked broken. "It doesn't matter. Maybe someday when the girls are off on their own, but not now."

"Well I'm not leaving Tacoma. We'll find her together, Darren."

I looked to Tara, who nodded at me. We often spoke without ever saying a word. "Yeah, Chief. Let's get out of this bar and go find your daughter so that we can back to ours."

"I appreciate that, MacKenzie, but take Tara home. Your mini gangster is waiting. Heaven help us all if she's hungry." His lips curled into a rare smile.

"Father to father, wasn't that what you said? I'm not finished until Sarah is safe, so we'd better hustle."

Chapter Seven

SLUMMIN' WITH A SAM'S TOWN MECHANIC

I'd flown back to Vegas on the police jet early that morning. Nothing had gone the way I'd hoped. So I was back at my old trailer with Grace in tow to see "Big Big Doggy."

Jake Tanner, my former next door neighbor and the closest thing I had to a best friend, had agreed to meet me there that afternoon.

"So remind me why you're not just putting in a new fridge?" He was the best mechanic I knew and could repair just about anything.

"Can it be fixed? I said I'd pay you."

He waved his hand in the air. "As if, even if you *are* fancy as fuck now. Get me into Oliver's dressing room before the fight and we'll call it good."

"Done," I said, mentally counting how many bodies I could allow my fighter to be distracted by on fight night.

"Cool. I'll need to order a new condenser for it. When did you say she's moving in?"

"Short term rental, not moving in." I couldn't bear the thought of selling the place, despite knowing we'd never live there again. Somehow that shabby piece of my past kept me grounded. "When in cools down," she said.

"So December," Jake said with a chuckle.

"I think next month. Be nice to her, but not *too* nice."

"No worries, I'm spoken for, I guess. But Cass said she's read all of her books, so she's excited to have her here. We can't believe she's actually going to be staying here."

"Yeah, it's nuts. But she sent Tara a DM about it a while back."

"She messaged Tara? Do you *still* ignore your social media?"

I nodded my head. "You know I hate that shit. But Oliver is pretty adamant that I start posting once we start promoting the gyms. Anyway, I guess this chick hunted us down because mine is the only unoccupied trailer in the whole place and her new series is going to be set here."

"Is she cute?"

"Settle down, Romeo. And I have no idea – I only agreed in the name of literature." I couldn't help but crack a rare smile at the thought of a romance writer spending her autumn in my shitty trailer, wedged between Jake-the-should-be-a-model and Becky the always-in-a-drama. She'd certainly have plenty of material to write about.

"Maybe she'll put us on book covers," Jake said, his fingers simulating the snap of a camera.

"You? For sure. But no one would ever put my banged-up gangster mug on one of those books. They're always pristine billionaires or motorcycle dudes. No one is gonna write a romance novel about an ex-con former gang banger. Hell, even worse, who would want to read about a guy totally devoted to his girl and his kid?"

"Everyone would, Mack." Jake cocked his head to one side, as if the thought intrigued him. "You know, normal guys who just happen to get into unlikely adventures. Just like us. Well, just like us with anaconda sized dicks maybe. They always have those in the steamy stuff Cassidy reads. Giant cocks that go all night long."

"Whatever, Bro. No one is going to read stories set in Sam's Town, no matter who she has on her covers or how prolific their massive members might be." I didn't bother to tell him that she'd actually said her book was about a modern-day Vegas vampire, Santino the Eternal or some shit.

He shrugged and plopped down on the floor. "So what the hell actually happened in Seattle?" he asked.

"Tacoma, actually. I found out there's a huge differ-ence. Sort of like Vegas and North Vegas – very different vibe."

"Okay, Tacoma then. The raid made the news here. It was buried with Raiders shit and another tourist hitting a jackpot at McCarran minutes before going home broke, but still. It looked mega."

Jake raised an eyebrow, waiting for the download from me. He was sitting cross-legged on my 70s shag carpet, a watchful green eye on Grace as she attempted to dress his massive Great Dane in doll's clothes.

I wasn't worried about Cerberus, his gentle giant of a dog. My own watchful gaze was on Grace – she liked to bite. But she had a natural way with animals, sort of like a creature-whisperer, so I suspected the playful-ish chomping habit extended only to humans.

I looked back at Jake, who was eager for my answer. "Well, yeah, it was huge. Local and state cops jumped in, I think even the FBI. The entire trafficking ring was brought down."

"So the docks are crime free? And Mack the cop is over?"

I had to laugh. The idea of me officially being on that

side of the law was absurd, no matter how straight and narrow I was walking. "No more cuffs for me, at least not in a non-bedroom setting. But crime free? Never. Panda works *with* the locals though, so as long as he doesn't cross the line they'll leave him alone."

"And as long as he pays them?"

I nodded. "Of course. But we missed the girl. The scum she's with got tipped off and they headed for Mexico, rumor has it."

"That blows. Once they get her across the border, she'll disappear."

I knew he was right. "Yeah, the Chief is already on his way down there. I told him I'd be there right after the fight. I know I'd move heaven and earth if it were Grace."

"Are you even allowed to cross the border with your record?" Jake's fingers ran through his blacker-than-a-Great-Basin-night hair.

"I am now. Apparently the powers that be felt like I kept my end of the deal and did some creative legal paper-work this morning."

"That's epic, Bro!"

I wasn't nearly as happy about it as I should have been. "Yeah, whatever. I didn't hold up my end of the deal. But once I bring his kid back from Mexico, then I'll be able to relax."

Jake laughed loud enough for Grace to shoot him a glare. "Mack MacKenzie, relax? Maybe when Death Valley freezes over."

I took a deep breath. "Yeah, well, maybe I'll be free of *that* shit anyway. But how about you? I saw Cassidy's new movie on a billboard at the airport. She still slummin' with a Sam's Town mechanic?"

Jake crawled over to Grace and Cerberus to help her put her Pooh Bear, Harold, on the dog's massive back. He glanced back toward me. "We're still hanging out, if that's what you mean. I don't fit into her Hollywood world though, never will. It's complicated."

"She's from here, Jake, same as us. Besides, you'll fit right in with them, pretty boy. Imagine how a guy like me feels walking red carpets with Oliver. It's fucking insane."

"I was dying laughing when ESPN had footage of you guys at that fight last month. Clearly Oliver got you in a suit but not so much the appropriate shoes. Cass said she was taking you over to the Boot Barn next time you're both in town at the same time."

I glanced down at my old beat-up black boots. "They're fine. Not everything needs to be all shiny and new. We can't all be perfect-looking Jake Tanners, after all. I mean at least Tara doesn't mind scars and scruff."

Jake was that guy that all the girls swooned over growing up, and still did. He had the classic sort of look that made you assume he was a celebrity, even though he was simply a broke auto mechanic who happened to be dating one. A decent one, at that. I liked Cassidy Lane, who was from Sam's Town the same us. I'd barely seen her after they broke up, but now that she was back in Jake's life whenever we managed to be in the same city it was like old times.

Jake glanced down at his phone. "Fuck, Bro. Ma just texted me this."

I walked over and froze at the image on his screen. "That's her! How the hell did your mother end up in Mexico?"

He shook his head. "No, this is at TGI's – just now she said. She waited on them and recognized Sarah from the news."

"Holy fucking shit, she's at Sam's Town? He took her

to a casino? Dammit, the Chief's probably to Yuma by now and she's right under our noses."

Jake was tapping hurriedly at his phone. "They left the restaurant, but Ma said they're still on the casino floor. She said to hurry."

Chapter Eight

A REAL MAN WHO SLURPED DOWN CINNAMON DRINKS IN THE MIDDLE OF THE DAY

"Hey Tony, what's happening, man?"

The massive guy in the standard casino security dark suit turned to face me. "MacKenzie! It's been ages since your criminal ass has been in here. Heard you were in town for the big fight. I always knew you'd make it outta here eventually."

"Thanks, Bro," I said with a tap on his huge arm. "Looks like you're staying clean?"

He nodded. "Yeah, I've gotta kid now and all. Sam's Town has been great about overlooking my past as long as I keep the floor quiet. You want some drink coupons? Well drinks only, but still."

"Nah, man, I don't…" Then I saw him. "Actually, yeah, thanks. Hey, that guy over at the bar. You ever seen him in here before?" Tony was former Saints & Sinners and knew everyone on this side of town.

He shook his head. "No, and he's on my shit list. Dude rolled in here with some clearly underage chick. When I asked her for ID she showed me some fake passport."

"What did you do?"

Tony shrugged. "I didn't really want to give her shit. She seemed nervous, afraid maybe."

"Of him?"

"Not really. More just antsy. I didn't confiscate her paperwork, but I did tell them she wasn't using it here. Dude wanted to drink fairly desperately, so she wandered off toward the shops."

"Do me a favor, buddy. Will you make sure she doesn't leave?"

With a deep breath, he cringed as if not wanting to get involved.

"She's the daughter of Chief Lane. That guy is bad news. I'm sorta doing him a personal favor."

Tony's eyes lit up. "Do you think you could put a good word in with me over at Metro? I know with my record I can't be a cop, but they have other stuff."

"Of course, man. And hey, we're always looking for good contract security over at the arena for fights. How about you come on out and give us a hand next week? It pays way better than this gig for sure."

"That'd be awesome, Mack. You think I could meet Oliver Martinez?"

"Naturally! I'll add you to the list." I mentally added yet another name to the growing list of favors I'd promised in my boss' name.

———

"Hey, watcha drinkin'?"

The slug's head slowly turned to face me. I sat at the bar, a flashing video poker machine in front of me. In proper man-spacing protocol, I'd left an empty stool in between us.

He stared at me for a few seconds, his dark eyes already

showing signs of inebriation. Finally he slurred, "Fireball."

Ah, a real man who slurped down cinnamon drinks in the middle of the day while idiotically stabbing his fingers at cards on a screen.

"Cool. The guy over there gave me these drink coupons. You want 'em?"

"Yeah, cool, thanks. I'm sorta running outta cash. Idiot bartender won't comp me much."

I signaled to the bartender. "Hey, Chuck, can my new friend here get another shot or two? Compliments of Tony." I'd known him since we were kids.

"Sure, Mack." He didn't even bother to take the pieces of paper.

The piece of shit next to me reached greedily for the alcohol. "Thanks, Mack. I'm Marco, by the way." With a sloppy turn of his wrist, he poured the generic Fireball down his throat.

I pointed to his screen. "Hold the Queen and the Jack." He was drunk, but I needed him completely immo-bilized.

As he struggled to find the right buttons to hold the cards I'd told him to, I slipped the first few drops into his second drink.

The machine made a clinging noise, and Marco smiled wide. "Thanks, dude! You play this?" He sipped at the second shot, clearly starting to feel the burn.

"Video poker? Nah, I live here. Where are you from?"

"Uh, nowhere. My girl and I are about to head to…" His head rolled as he fought the urge to pass out.

"Keep the spades. Yeah, those four."

He struggled to focus on the glorified video game in front of him. "Oh, uh, but the 2-3-4…"

Marco leaned to the side, and I was sure he was going to fall. I reached to steady him, pointing to the video poker machine. "You've gotta play fast, Bro. That's the only way to win. Go for the flush."

As he poked at the lighted buttons in front of him, I emptied the little bottle into his drinks. It was one of the little tools from my past I always carried in my pocket.

The machine clanged wildly again, and Marco smiled at his winning hand. "Thanks, dude. This will help cover my tab. But I'm about to get a giant payout upstairs, so it's cool."

"Upstairs?" I pointed to his shot, hoping he had enough coordination left to finish it.

Marco sipped at the shot, half of it rolling down his ugly chin. "Yeah, my girl is gonna take one for the team and hook us up with some righteous cash."

"She's an escort?" I asked, hoping to get some answers from him before he started puking.

"Nice word for whore?" he slurred, spit starting to spew from his swollen lips.

"Where *is* Sarah?" My steely eyes bore into his watery ones. Despite his stupor, somewhere in his brain something clicked.

"How do you…you know her name…who are you?" His head bobbed, coming inches from hitting the video poker machine before fighting its way upright once again.

"No one you need to fuck with." And with that, he collapsed onto the bar, cinnamon scented bile pouring from his mouth.

I signaled to the bartender. "Hey, Chuck, I think this guy is down for the count. You think Tony could have him taken down to the drunk tank?"

"Sure thing, Mack," he said with a nod. A guy passed out in his own body fluid in the middle of a weekday afternoon was nothing new to an off-the-Strip casino bartender. He'd seen it all.

After cashing Marco out and leaving the voucher for Chuck as a tip, I tapped out a text for backup and went to find Sarah.

———

She was sitting at one of those tiny round tables at Starbucks, nervously looking around.

"Sarah! Hi. Do you remember me?"

Sarah startled at hearing her name. "Uh…?" Confused, she stared at me.

"Marco sent me over. He was feeling a little…"

"Drunk," she said.

I nodded. "Yeah, I'm Shawn the Snake. Remember I was with y'all out in Tacoma?"

She searched my face. "I'm sorry, it was all crazy up there. I don't remember you."

I shrugged. "Yeah, it was nuts. I didn't realize anyone else got out of it until I saw Marco at the bar a few minutes ago. He's feeling sick and asked me to help you with the job."

I could tell she didn't believe me. "You were in Tacoma? How'd you get around all those cops?"

Smart girl, testing my facts, I thought. Luckily, I *was* in Tacoma although on the right side of the law for once. "I hid in a shipping container full of Dungeness crab. You know, those massive ones out on that putrid water? The rusty brown ones?"

Sarah tilted her to one side, a faint grin raising the corners of her delicate mouth. "That's funny! We got out in some trout that same way. It took me all morning to get rid of the smell!"

I held up my hand, hoping she wouldn't recognize the Saints & Sinners logo inked onto it. "See that? That's where those pinchin' assholes got a piece of me." The scar was old, but she didn't seem to care. I'd given her enough details to prove to her that I was there. Later, I'd find out that I was lucky that she didn't know that we were well out of crab season.

She relaxed a little and slurped at her frozen espresso drink. "Well, after I do this trick Marco and I will be set cash-wise. We're headed to Ensenada the second I scrub the rich guy's stink off of me."

I leaned into her. "I don't think Marco's going anywhere, sweetheart. He's headed down to County to sleep it off."

She gulped as her palms drifted to her flushed face. I knew she was confused, lost even.

I pointed to the keycard in front of her on the sticky table. "You don't have to do that, Sarah. I mean, you could go home. I'll drive you."

Her eyes narrowed at me. "No! I love Marco and he loves me."

"Guys who love you don't sell you." I pointed to her small neck. "Or leave marks like that."

Her hands instinctively went to the red marks in various stages of healing on her skin. It clearly happened regularly.

"He just gets agitated sometimes. He's mostly sweet. And he's never had me work before. It's just we need the cash to get out of the country and what this guy will pay for young blondes will set us up for a long time."

"Do you know who the guy is?" I was ready to slice him open with my trusty blade.

She shook her head. "No, but he's some sort of state politician. He made us meet him way out here in this shithole because he's doing some rally in the ballroom tomorrow."

I let out a deep sigh and reached for the keycard. "Okay, then, I guess since he's shitfaced as fuck, I'm your muscle. What floor we going to?"

She looked relieved and terrified at the same time. "He's up in one of those cheesy jacuzzi suites up on the top floor. Marco said it was all the way on the end on the left."

I glanced at my phone, scratching my head at the text from Ava.

Hey, great news about the girl. I'm in Tacoma tho. Went back to hang with Panda (don't ask!) but I sent her there with someone else. They should be there by now.

I knew if a pack of cops rolled in and grabbed Sarah, she'd just runaway again. It had to be her decision. I'd asked Ava to come since they knew each other, but I'd failed to actually make sure Ava was back in town. I certainly didn't expect her to be off having a tryst with Panda of all people.

Sarah finally spoke. "Let's just get this over with then."

Her words were decisive, but her hands shook as she pushed back from the table.

———

The walk seemed to take forever across the garish, worn carpet of the casino floor toward the bank of elevators that led to the hotel rooms.

I inhaled a deep wave of smoke, semi-missing the days

when I indulged in that incidious habit, as I scanned the casino floor. And then, as I reached for my phone to share our location, she grabbed my hand.

"Just a minute," she said. "I, uh, maybe…is there another way?"

"Another way to…?"

"To get the cash. Can we just, um, steal it or something? I really *don't* want to do this."

I nodded. "Yeah, I get it." Relief flooded me – she was starting to wake up.

I turned to face her. "Let's just get out of here, Sarah."

The color drained from her face. "I can't go back to Marco without the money. He'll beat the shit out of me. *Again*."

Deep down, at that moment, I knew Marco would never touch another girl again. I put my hand on her shoulder. "You really want to be with that loser?"

Her eyes met mine. "Who are you? Really? Because you're *not* one of them."

"I used to be, sort of. I *was* in Tacoma, but I was there with your dad."

And then, faster than a roadrunner crossing Boulder Highway, she pulled away from me and ran.

Just before the wall of doors that led to outside, she froze. "Mom?"

Tears poured down her face as her mother ran toward her. "Baby girl! You're safe now."

Sarah melted into her mother's arms. "I'm so sorry, Mommy, I really thought he loved me. I want to come home, but Dad will be so pissed. All that stuff in Tacoma was because of *me*."

Her mother, Estelle, held her closer. "No, baby. It's all okay now. He's on his way back from the border now."

"He was going to Mexico?"

Estelle nodded. "Of course, Sarah. We were never going to let you live in danger. You're our flesh and blood."

"I thought I loved him, but now…I just want to go home."

Tara had come in with Sarah's mother, and finally caught up to the three of us.

"Ava called me and asked me to bring Estelle," she said to me.

"She couldn't have sent a cop?"

"We were afraid Sarah would run if she saw police. Wasn't that *your* plan?"

"My plan was for Ava, who Sarah knows, to bring her mother over here. My plan was *not* for *you* to put yourself in danger yet again."

"Well, Shawn, you know damn well I'm not some fragile damsel in distress who's going to sit on the sidelines. We're a team, my dear future husband."

I wrapped my arms around her. "I'm fully aware of how totally badass the women in my life are."

"Speaking of which, let's go get Grace. I think she's nibbled the hell out of Jake and Oliver is getting restless back at Red Rock. There's some big party at the pool tonight for all of his supporters, and he said you'd better be there."

I buried my face in her hair. "I will, I swear. I'll be back in a bit."

"Shawn, this is over. Let's just go back to normal life. You've sacrificed enough. It's up to them now to heal with their daughter."

I'd leave Marco for the Chief to deal with as he saw fit, but I knew there was no way I was leaving the monster upstairs to prey on anyone else.

I glanced at the plastic hotel room keycard in my hand.

"I love you, Tara, always. But I have to take care of this one last thing before I leave Sam's Town."

THE END

———

This Sam's Town novella has been an extended version of the short story *HUSTLE*, published in Tempted and Tantalizing's *CUFFED* anthology.

If you want more of Mack's story, be sure to read the first two books of the *Sam's Town* series, *REDEMPTION* and *SACRIFICE*. Watch for the conclusion, *GRACE*, to release soon.

Have you read the beginning,
REDEMPTION?

One bad boy who suddenly becomes a single father.

One unexpected romance with his new daughter's fiery social worker.

One man who finally finds a chance at redemption by two bonds of love that sink deeper than he ever imagined…

———

I never wanted her. I never wanted anyone, for that matter. But here she is, dropped on my shabby doorstep one sweltering Vegas afternoon. My newborn daughter Grace is beautiful, perfect, and apparently mine thanks to a meaningless fling with someone I barely know.

I want to change my life for her, but I'm terrified. Can I, ex-con Shawn "Mack" MacKenzie, ever get it together enough for them to let me keep my precious daughter? God knows I'll try, but it won't be easy. The odds are against us, but I am determined to sacrifice everything for love and ultimately, hopefully, a chance at redemption.

I Stuck It In You Like Once

REDEMPTION preview

Shawn "Mack" MacKenzie

I opened the door of my hand-me-down trailer before she knocked. Used to listening for danger, my ears were trained to detect the telltale creak of the about-to-fall-apart wooden stairs.

"Yeah?" That was the only greeting that tweaker chick got from me that scorching Vegas afternoon.

"Mack?"

I glanced up and down. She was some strung-out bleached blonde, tall and skinny. *Too* skinny and too pale – after a decade of selling drugs, I knew an addict when I saw one. Even worse, next to her on the porch was a car seat, its contents covered in some sort of tiny blanket.

"You fucking came to my *house*? I don't deal anymore, baby. Turn around and get off my damn porch."

"It's Misty. Don't you remember me?"

I squinted at her in the harsh sunlight. The eyes I recognized, maybe the nose. "What, did I deal to you or something? I told you, I don't do that anymore."

"I know. Security, that's your thing. That and making people pay - Dollar Loan Center and the Pink Kitty, right?"

"Who the fuck are you?" I could feel my blood pressure rising faster than the heat index.

"Misty Magic, from the Pink Kitty. We hooked up nine and a half months ago." She reached down and pulled the flimsy blanket from the car seat. Little blue eyes looked up at me, barely able to focus.

"Misty?" I glanced from her to the baby, trying to remember the one night I'd spent with a random stripper from the club. Not even a night, really. It was a few hours. But she'd been different then: beautiful, curvy, and the thing I liked about her the most – sassy. She definitely wasn't the washed out shell of a human that was currently standing in front of me.

"Please, Mack, don't let my parents have her. They'll destroy her soul like they did mine." She glanced over her shoulder nervously. "And most of all, keep her safe. From *them*, from me."

I took a deep breath and glanced at the pink little being on my porch. "Misty, listen, I'm not sure exactly what you're implying…"

"She's your daughter."

Her calloused hand reached in a plastic grocery bag and pulled out a piece of paper. I scanned the birth certificate. Sure enough, this lunatic had truly done it.

Name: Grace Olivia MacKenzie

. . .

Then further down:

Mother: Melissa Ann Warner
Father: Shawn Patrick MacKenzie

"Who's Melissa?"

She rolled her dilated eyes. "Me, idiot. You thought my given name was Misty Magic?"

"I didn't care," I admitted. "Listen, Melissa, Misty, who-the-fuck-ever – I don't have any money, if that's what you're after."

"I'm *after* a home for my daughter. *Our* daughter. Away from drugs, pimps, and my evil parents. You're all she has now."

"We both know she's not mine." But, as I looked at Grace Olivia again, I knew she was. "I stuck it in you like once and you want me to believe you had my kid?"

"*Four* times, don't you remember? And *you* were the sober one."

Another eye roll from her had me remembering this chick. Less than a year ago she was a gorgeous, take-no-shit moneymaker at the club. And now she was just sad. I felt the familiar stab of remorse at how many like her I'd sold drugs to.

"You were probably with a ton of guys during that same time. Why do you think she's mine?"

"I was with zero guys, asshole. You think stripper equals slut?"

I shook my head. I did not think that. But I also did not think I'd ever be the parent of some gorgeous baby with

Misty Magic from the Pink Kitty. "I didn't mean it that way, *Melissa*."

She cringed at hearing her given name, shaking me off as I tried to hand her the birth certificate. "Keep it, you'll need it. Listen, Mack, I tried to stay clean when I was knocked up and she's healthy, but this last month I'm off the rails again. Even worse, the pimp I've been working for these last couple of days is threatening to sell her. Please...?"

"Are you positive she's mine? If you're pulling one on me, they'll find you in a wash out in the Mojave."

"I'm sure. Tell them to do a DNA test. She's yours! Look at her – how can you deny it?"

I forced myself to look at the little being again. Giant blue eyes stared back at me. *My* eyes. She definitely had my eyes, but she also had my distinctive hair, my mother's nose, and the stripper-turned-user-turned-whore's chin. She was the most perfect thing I'd ever seen.

"Okay, so say she is mine. There has to be a better home for her than here." I waved my hand at my falling-apart trailer in one of the few trailer parks in the city – right under the shadow of the once-luxurious Sam's Town Gambling Hall. It wasn't the ghetto, but it wasn't exactly utopic suburbia, either.

"She belongs with you," she said, glancing over her shoulder.

"Do you need help with these guys?" I asked. A beat-up black Lincoln was hovering down the street and it was starting to roll up toward us.

"No, I'm good. Just please – take care of Grace. No matter what, don't let my family near her."

And with, that she turned and ran – away from me, away from the pimps in the black car, but most of all, she ran from our daughter.

I chased after her, but when I turned the corner she was gone. Living at the intersection of Boulder Highway and Nellis, traffic was choked up and she could have been anywhere. So there I stood, sweating and shirtless, her words echoing in my brain. *Take care of our daughter.*

Shit! I'd left the baby alone!

But she wasn't alone. And she was wailing with attitude – I couldn't believe such a tiny thing could have lungs like that.

In the unpaved parking area in front of our trailers, a giant Great Dane was bouncing up and down, clearly distraught at the newborn's discomfort.

"Bro, watch your dog!" I howled at my neighbor, Jake Tanner.

"Oh please," he said as he bounced the baby in his arms. "Cerberus loves babies."

"And stop fucking shaking her!"

"I'm soothing her, Bro. My family is Irish, remember? Babies everywhere!"

"Whatever, you're not supposed to shake them. Even I know that."

Jake ignored me and walked in small circles in the gravel, his voice in some shushing sing-song tone.

"She's wet and hungry. Whose is she?" he asked.

"Apparently mine." I sat down on the steps and pulled out the tattered birth certificate. "At least some chick said so."

"She just dropped a baby on your doorstep? Dude, that's like stuff that only happens in a movie."

"Story of my life," I said with a sigh. I'd certainly not exactly done things the traditional way. "The thing is, she might actually not be lying."

Jake looked into Grace's howling face, his eyes narrowing as he examined her delicate features. "She certainly has your temper, although I doubt she's done time for manslaughter and shit."

"Very funny, asshole."

He squinted at the baby one more time, and then looked over at me.

"Well?" I asked. "Is there a resemblance or whatever? And if you make another fucking joke, I'll be back in prison after I break your face."

He chuckled. "My face is a masterpiece – you'd never ruin it. Break a leg, maybe. An arm, sure. But not my pretty face. And yeah, she's *totally* your mini-me."

The whole thing was surreal. A howling baby that was probably mine, his gentle giant of a dog licking the kid's feet, and my pretty-boy pal Jake Tanner desperately trying to quiet her. With a deep breath, I stood up and reached for her.

"Don't sweat on her, and for fuck's sake don't squeeze her too hard," he scolded as I wrapped the tiny thing in my massive arms.

"Squeeze her?" I said, instinctively pulling her close – ignoring the sweat warning.

"Yeah, you're like the fucking Hulk – I could see you not knowing your strength and POOF, there goes baby." Jake laughed, always more amused at his constant jokes than anyone else.

"Look, she likes this," I said as Grace nuzzled into me, her tiny head settling into the hollow of my chest like she was meant to be there. My right hand wrapped around her, and I knew in that moment that love at first sight was completely real. I'd only known her for fifteen minutes, and she was my entire world.

"Of course she does – skin to skin. They like that." He reached into the back pocket of his ripped jeans and pulled out his phone. "Oh my God, this is like the best picture. Stand over against Becky's fence and hold her just like that."

"Not now, I need to figure out who to call…"

"It'll take two seconds. Think of it as evidence or whatever."

"I didn't commit a crime, motherfucker."

"Maybe we shouldn't swear around her…she's a kid and shit."

I glared at him.

"Gawd, I'm kidding. You're always so intense. C'mon, a couple of quick pics and then let's document the car seat here and stuff. You know, in case the cops come."

"Cops? I've had enough of that shit to last me a lifetime. I mean, I almost did a *lifetime*." Grace, now silent and sleeping in my arms, made a little noise and I pulled her even closer to me.

"I think she likes my heartbeat."

"Yeah, it's like it's meant to be."

"But Jake, I'm no father! I mean shit, this kid deserves better than some ex-con." I glanced around the parking lot of the trailer park. It wasn't the worst part of the city, but it wasn't exactly Henderson or Summerlin with the good schools and the sort of opportunities she deserved.

"Okay, then, call 911 and let them take her." He shot me a smirk, fully confident that I had no intention of doing that.

"Well, I do have a birth certificate and I'm named as the father. Mandy seemed pretty confident that—"

"Mandy?"

"The mother, douchebag."

71

He shook his head at me in disbelief. "*Misty*, not Mandy. You might learn the name of the mother of your kid."

"How do *you* know?"

With an eye roll, he said, "I was there the night you hooked up with her. She's been over at Sam's Town playing Blackjack, pregnant as fuck. Are you that oblivious?"

Jake pointed his phone at us and said, "Smile like one of those Instagram assholes."

Of course I ignored him. I didn't fucking smile. Ever.

Grace moved a little, her tiny bare chest rising and falling against mine as I held her.

"Your hand is almost bigger than her whole body." Jake was snapping pictures, turning his phone in every direction to get the best light.

I looked down, and he was right. My hand, covered in the ink that told the story of my life, was a stark contrast to this small, delicate being. And yet, I knew she was a part of me.

"Perfect!" he said. "I'm tagging you in this one."

"Tagging?"

"Oh my God, use social media once in a while, Mack. You know, so your family can see her."

"No," I said too loudly. Grace stirred, a tiny cry starting to form, and I bounced her a little until she settled again.

"Don't shake her," he teased.

"Seriously, Jake, I don't want anyone to know about this yet. Especially not family, okay?"

"Sure," he said, swiping through the pictures on his phone. "I'll text you these, though. That last one is completely IG worthy."

"IG?"

He sighed again. "Jesus, whatever. Forget it." Glancing at his watch, he reached down and grabbed Cerberus' collar. "I gotta go – I'm driving Ma home this afternoon from the casino."

"Wait, what am I supposed to do?"

He shrugged. "Did she come with a kit or anything?"

"Like instructions?"

"Like a diaper bag? Food? Any of that shit? I mean she's not even fucking dressed."

I shook my head. "No, this is all."

"Well you've got her papers, get her registered and shit I guess. But first maybe Becky knows what to do. She's had like twenty kids or something."

"And that many maybe daddies," I joked. My next-door neighbor, Becky Donner, seemed to always be pregnant yet we'd never actually seen her with a man of any sort.

"Cool. Thanks, Bro." I walked past him and his giant dog toward my front door. It was far too hot to keep Grace outside much longer – or at least, it seemed like that should be true. Even worse, her diaper was soaked.

"Oh," Jake said, glancing over his shoulder. "Do you want me to take Thug until you figure it all out?"

"What? Why would…?"

"Pit bull and a baby," he shrugged.

"Thug is a million years old and won't even chase a fly. You know he's the biggest pussy ever."

He nodded. "Oh yeah, I know, but I'm just saying he might knock her over or whatever."

"I think we've got some time to worry about all of that – for now, she's not exactly crawling across the floor."

"True, true," he said as he walked the few steps back to his own trailer.

———

Want more? Sam's Town Book One, REDEMPTION, is available on Amazon Kindle or wherever paperbacks are sold online.

Taken at the Boxing Bag

TARA THE SCREWED

SACRIFICE Preview

"I'm glad you came! I nearly screamed when I saw you text me about happy hour."

I glanced around the crowded restaurant, relieved to see no sign of the three men pursuing me. "I didn't want to miss the fight. Besides, I do what I want."

"You go, girl. But hey, I did hear some rumors that Hank is in town." Maddie stared at me from over her menu. "Apparently the body out by the Binion silver was just some washed-up mobster from the 60s."

"Oh, cool," I said, trying to sound disinterested.

"But some guy at the courthouse said he definitely saw Hank this morning filling up some blue car at that 7-Eleven near your old condo."

I glanced around the restaurant, determined to avoid the topic. "Why the freak did you want to meet at Applebee's?" It was a stark departure from our former happy hour haunts.

"One dollar margaritas, yo!"

I ran my finger across the sticky table. "Since when do you care about bargains?"

She shrugged. "The guy I'm seeing is a bit…"

"Cheap?"

"Short on funds. But he's so sweet! We come here a lot."

"So wait, you're actually dating this guy? More than once?"

"Don't tease me, but we've been going out for a month."

"No bad sex stories? This guy must be a machine."

"I wouldn't know," she said with a wide grin. "We haven't yet."

"Holy shizz," I said. I'd never heard Maddie talk about any sort of relationship. "Do I get to meet him?"

"Soon, but I'm not sure you're going to like it."

Before I could ask why, she was back on the Hank topic like it was the latest TMZ dish. "Seriously, Tara, if Hank is back in town, you need to be careful. He nearly killed you!"

To my best friend, and most of Vegas, Hank fled town after we'd had an argument that became physical. The story explained his disappearance and my visible injuries. My father's contacts and Metro PD signed off on that version before his body was even cold.

"I heard he has a new chick. Someone told my dad that he was leaving for Mexico." I did my very best to sound nonchalant, even though inside I was praying she'd let it go. I was a terrible liar. "Besides, I need to get a few last things from the condo and finally put it on the market."

I couldn't care less about selling my former home that was still being paid for from Hank's hefty bank accounts. What I really wanted was to find any clue as to why he was haunting me.

That and some clothes, I'd hoped. Besides a few things

from the cleaners rattling around in my car, I had pretty much nothing with me. And I had no intention of leaving Vegas until everything was resolved, once and for all.

"Still, Tara, you should be careful," Maddie warned. "And what's this thing I heard about you engaging in lascivious fornication at the gym earlier?"

Of course, at that very moment, our embarrassed waiter appeared to take our order.

"Spill it!" she demanded as soon as the nervous twenty-something server was gone.

"How did you know?" It had only been hours since my knees had hit the tile of the men's shower.

"*Everyone* is talking about it. That's a classy gym, you slutty whore."

"No one is talking about it. Sometimes I think you have me bugged."

"Not a bad idea, actually. But I need the details of this secret tryst between you and the felon."

"It wasn't like that. It was more like…angry sex, I guess. Wait until I tell you what I found at his old trailer!"

"Tell me about the torrid sex-capade first. I need a great scene for my latest story."

"Oh, another novel?" Maddie never actually *wrote* any of these books, she just imagined them. Over the course of our friendship, she'd come up with thousands of story ideas but as far as I knew, had yet to actually type more than a few words.

"Yes! The best one yet. *Taken at the Boxing Bag*, I think that's the perfect title."

"Well, it didn't happen there. We sort of fought, argued, then I tried to punch him."

"Always good to take out relationship angst with your fists…not."

"It wasn't like that. It was actually cathartic and we——"

"Skip to the fucking."

"Romantic."

"I'm actually shooting for erotic. So how'd you end up in the men's locker room?"

"How *did* you find out? I'm not telling you one more thing until you come clean."

"Andy MacKenzie told me."

"You're talking to his brother?"

"Dating, actually. Don't you dare scold me!"

I did *not* see that one coming. "Shawn told Andy about the…the shower?"

"Apparently my beloved Andrew was taking a shit while you were having your holes drilled by his murderous brother."

Our poor waiter arrived at that very moment, his face as red as a tourist's skin in late July.

"She's joking," I said as he dropped the food and nearly ran from our table.

"You seriously need to learn to whisper!" I scolded as I stabbed a fork into my orange chicken.

"Okay, so give me the details," she said, her mouth full of salad. "I'll write it in a scene for my new hit book, *Screwed in Summerlin*."

I sipped at my watered-down Long Island. The truth was, I was dying to tell someone and ecstatic to be engaged in girl-talk with my best friend again.

"Okay, so it went like this. We had some angry words and he stormed off to the showers. So I snuck in there and did stuff."

"Did stuff?"

"Yeah, you know, I did *things*. Anyone could have walked in!"

She slapped the table. "You cannot tell it like that, Tara! Yawn city!"

"Fine. I gave him a blow job and then he did stuff to me."

"Riveting."

"You're the supposed writer. How would you say it?"

Her eyes went wide as she slurped down the rest of her drink like the thirsty girl that she was.

"It was a hot Vegas afternoon when I stormed into the steamy locker room, my loins on fire from the desire that raged from within."

"That might be a bit dramatic."

"All these scenes are like that! Seriously, Tara, you need make your reading material a bit hotter."

"I'll make note of that. But it really was scorching! I went in fully dressed and just…did it!"

"Did it. Descriptive. I'd say it like this…"

The waiter set down two more drinks, fleeing the scene faster than a Baptist accidentally at a Zumanity performance.

"In a wave of pure lust, I tore off my clothes and burst into—"

"I was dressed, actually. I just opened the shower door and walked in and dropped to my knees—"

"Tara, shush. Let me get back to your story. In a fit of lust, I dropped to my knees in front of his massive fifteen-inch cock…"

"Oh my god, stop. Fifteen inches? Who would even want that?"

"You can't have an average penis in an erotic story, Einstein. It has to be the biggest tool ever in existence."

"Yeah but I think that would hurt."

"No one cares about practicality, Tara. In truth, the best sex I've ever had was with this guy who was literally hung like a clit."

"Now there's an image I won't be able to get out of my brain."

"Seriously! It was *small*. Even better, small and uncut – like a turtleneck on a Vienna sausage. But he tried so hard! I miss Edgar and his mini wrinkly dick. It was like one of those creepy hairless cats."

"Why'd you stop seeing him?"

"He found Jesus. I only hope he prays for that thing to grow. But back to your sex scene."

"Can we talk about the weather instead?"

"Always, it's Vegas, but after the scene. Seriously, this is going to hit the *New York Times* Bestseller list."

"I don't see a lot of fifteen-inch penis stories on *that* list."

"Okay, fine, but it'll be an Amazon International Bestseller. So the scene continues – I was on my knees in front of his massive member, our skin so slippery that I had to hang on to his rock hard—"

"Don't you think *rock hard* is overused?"

"No, that's how you do it."

"What if you said something like harder than a pervert at the AVN Expo?" I giggled to myself at the very thought of the time Maddie dragged me to Vegas' biggest porn convention.

"Um, I'll do the writing, thanks. Our skin was so slippery that I had to grasp onto his rock hard ass, my slippery finger thrusting inside him as he moaned, his head thrown back in sheer ecstasy."

"I hadn't thought of that," I said, pondering the idea of a soapy finger. "I wonder if he would like that sort of thing?"

"This isn't sex ed, stop interrupting. It should go like this – with my eager finger stroking him, his juices exploded down my—"

"If you say juices one more time, I'm leaving."

"Fine, what would you say?"

"Semen, ejaculate, possibly just that he..."

"That's too damn clinical. Okay, if we can't use the j-word we'll use...salty seed."

"I nearly just vomited in my mouth."

"We'll move on then to the climax. Is that how it ended? With you all sad and soaked on the cold tile floor?"

I shook my head. "Of course not. But I started to worry about someone coming in. When I was kneeling, no one could see me. But afterward, he lifted me up and peeled off my wet workout pants."

"Ah, sexy. You really should record this. After I swallowed his salty seed, his strong arms lifted me as my designer leggings fell to my ankles."

"Well, no, actually they were those Target ones that never fit right. It was like when you try to pull off two-sizes-too-small Spanx when you're all sweaty. We finally just gave up and he pushed me against the wall with the ten-dollar leggings puddled at my knees."

"Yeah, that is just sad. But no worries! We aren't going for reality here, Tara. We *are* going for the hottest fucking sex scene ever. It goes like this: my naked skin coated by the warm water, he pressed me against the shower wall and pounded into my tightness with his rock hard cock—"

"Didn't he just finish? And you used rock hard *again*."

"In these scenes they can just go and go...never a waiting period. Like they are insta-hard and consta-hard. So he pounds you again and again as you howl."

"I was quiet, didn't want to get caught. And no, it was just...you know...mouth."

"Shut up. It goes like this: I howled like a coyote hunting jackrabbits as he pounded into me again and again, his massive—"

"Maddie!" There was a man standing behind her as her narration grew more and more explicit. And *loud*.

"Don't interrupt. It's about to get to the third money shot. I came like a shotgun as he plowed into my tight pussy over and over, the inferno of our lust exploding like a…"

"Maddie! Stop!"

"Not now, they're about to come. Like a super nova of burning love, our bodies driven by an endless need for fanatical fucking—"

"Madalyn, I haven't seen you in church lately."

Never have I seen my best friend blush – but her skin was burning far hotter than her absurd sex scene. She turned slowly to face the man standing behind her.

"Reverend Dimsdale! Imagine seeing you here."

"One dollar Long Islands," he said, no hint of humor in his tone. "Do you remember my wife, Caroline? She's missed you at choir practice."

Maddie jumped up to shake the woman's hand.

"It's nice to run into you, perhaps we'll see you in church on Sunday," Caroline said with a grin. "Oh, and finish that scene - I want that book!"

———

Be sure to read the entire Sam's Town Series!

I Thought You Were My Pizza

A Sam's Town Preview: Jake's Story (Unpublished)

"Jake, I need your help," she said that afternoon.

"Hey, Cass," was all I could come up with. I leaned into the doorframe, wishing I'd turned off my The Walking Dead marathon before I'd answered. "I thought you were my pizza." It was true, I did.

I hadn't seen her in two years. I mean, not in person. Everyone has seen her—she's all over. Cassidy Lane, star of stage and screen, was the hottest thing since jello shots. She was also my first love, my high school sweetheart, and the one that got away.

"What ya need? Like car problems or somethin'?"

She just stared at me. That's how it all started; with her standing on the concrete block porch in front of my shitty trailer. That's how we fell back into the toxic vortex that will always be Jake and Cass.

———

I'd worked twelve hours straight that entire week. The garage was running some special coupon deal in the mailer that goes out every week, and we were swamped. When I finally clocked out, two radiators and an engine block later, I planned to dive into Netflix, a six-pack of Bud, and a pizza with extra sausage. I hadn't even taken a shower when she knocked on my door and I'm sure I smelled worse than the zombies on my small TV. In ripped jeans, barefoot, wearing a torn wife beater t-shirt with grease on my face was not how I'd dreamed of seeing Cass again, that's for sure.

"Can I come in?" Oh God, she did not just ask that.

"Uh, I'm kinda busy, ya know. I just got home from work and all. How 'bout we catch a drink in an hour or so? The bar over at Sam's Town does four dollar well drinks at happy hour." She just stared at me. It seemed to be a theme. For six years I'd had my tongue buried in her as much as possible, and now she was someone that I used to know.

"Jake, please. I'll only take a minute. I don't have time to—"

I glanced toward the street. No one was around to see her, but her shiny Mercedes convertible would catch attention for sure, especially next to my dented truck. I held the door open and let her pass.

"It's a mess, I'm sorry, it's been crazy and—"

She cut me off and sailed by me into my dark living room. "Where's Cerberus?"

"Oh, yeah, he's with my ma. It got rough over there where she is and I've been working such long hours. I grab him on the weekends."

"It would have been nice to see him." My Great Dane loved Cass - but then again, everyone loved Cass. My dog, my mom, and even my sister - and that bitch doesn't like anybody.

Her eyes darted around my tiny metal home. "Yeah,

I Thought You Were My Pizza

uh, it's a wreck. Have a seat if you want, but the dog hair, uh…"

"It's you. My house would be trashed if I didn't have three maids." She blushed, embarrassed to be rich. More specifically, she was ashamed to be rich in her old neighborhood, with her old still-broke boyfriend. Like a delicate bird, she perched herself on the very edge of my sofa- a hand-me-down from my dead grandmother, like the trailer and the rest of the furnishings.

"It's been forever. What do you want? Not me, I'm guessing."

Those pale cornflower blue eyes met mine. God, why did she have to be so beautiful? Couldn't she be more horrible so I could forget her?

"Do you have a tuxedo?" she asked, the pink blush blooming on her perfect cheeks once again.

———

Cass

Going to see Jake Tanner was not my idea. I had a new life in LA, a role in a hit movie, a famous, handsome boyfriend, and was up for best supporting actress in the Golden Cinema Awards. Life was good, I was on top, and had left my old Sam's Town neighborhood in Vegas behind. And Jake - Jake was an old memory.

Except, none of it was what it seemed. I was broke, despite all the shiny things. The car and the house weren't paid for, and I was deep in debt from the dresses, the travel, the lifestyle in general. Matt sure didn't help me at all with cash, and he was rolling in it. I'd made decent money on my first film, but the last one, the one I was up for an award for, was indie and despite the big-name cast and the prestige, I was paid very little.

Even worse, Matt Scully, the handsome leading man taking Hollywood by storm, had dumped me the day before. To be more specific, he broke up with me the day before an awards show - one where I was a nominee. He didn't even do it in person. I'd love to say he sent a text, but it was worse than that - he had his assistant send a text to break up with me.

The show was televised across the globe, and this year it was held in my hometown of Las Vegas. I was already in town when he canned me. I did something I'm not proud of. I groveled. I called him; he ignored the call so I texted him. Please, Matt, just this one awards show - I can't go alone. I promise I'll never ask for anything again. He never answered the text, but he did take the time to block me on all of his social media accounts.

No, it wasn't my idea to leave the Strip and show up at Jake's door. It was Mom's.

I ran home that morning crying, crying to my mommy like I do when I'm upset. She held me in her arms on her velvet couch. "It'll be okay," she said as she stroked my hair. "You don't need him."

"I do need him," I argued.

"Cass, he was an asshole."

"I know."

"Did you love him?"

"No."

"Did you like him?"

"Not really. But I wanted to like him. And now, I have no date for the biggest thing that's ever happened to me."

"Just breathe," she said, in that reassuring way that always talks me down from the ledge.

"I'll take you, Mom. You can walk the carpet with me."

"I already have a seat at the table, but no you will not walk the red carpet with your mother. You need a hot man, you need someone to make the flashes go crazy."

"It's too late, ma. It's tonight and it's not like we're in LA."

"Cassie Lane, you will dry those tears and get off your ass and get yourself a pretty escort."

"Huh?" I sat up and looked her in the eye.

"You need the type of guy that would make Matt Scully look like a fool. A real man - a ridiculously good-looking one. The kind of man that everyone stares at and thinks he must be famous with that face."

"Jake? I haven't spoken to Jake in forever. The last time...it wasn't good. There's no way. Besides, what happens when the paparazzi gets wind that my date is a felon?"

"You are stubborn. Jake looks like a star, and him being blue-collar, urban, broke - it plays into the fantasy of uptown girl meets downtown boy. Just like in the movie you're nominated for. It's perfect, Cassie."

She was right. The media would eat it up - life imitating art. That was very near the plot of my movie, Love Runs Free. And Jake - he was beautiful, but also beautifully flawed. And together - we were like Superman and Kryptonite. The chemistry, the supernova of our love was so explosive, so all-encompassing, that it consumed us both. The last time we slept together, long after our breakup, I cried. We were so perfect together and yet at the same time we managed to always rip each other open.

I couldn't be with Jake again. But, it might be nice to see him, and maybe we could be friends for this one night, the biggest night of my career. I dusted off my pride and drove over to where he lived - the same place he grew up, his grandmother's trailer.

I stood on the porch for a long time, too nervous to knock. It looked the same as I remembered, no better and no worse. The white paint was peeling, and the screens were ripped, but it always looked like that. I turned to leave; I couldn't do it. The giant, hulking presence of the Sam's Town Casino a street away reminded me of all the nights we spent sneaking around, of all the times we had with our friends tearing up those streets, of all of it. And without thinking, I spun around and my fist struck his door.

When he opened it, and his eyes caught mine, I felt as if the air was being sucked from my lungs.

———

Jake

"A tux? Uh, I haven't worn one since senior prom." Cass was often all over the place, but she was really confusing me. But I didn't want her to leave - I'd missed her like an addict misses their fix. And yeah, I do know what that feels like.

"Oh, it's fine. I'm sure we can work around that. Listen, I need a favor, a huge one."

I didn't answer. What the actual fuck could she need from me?

"So I'm up for that award thing tonight, and it's here in Vegas, and well, I kind of don't have a date."

Of course I knew about the award—I already planned to be glued to the TV to watch her - after my zombie marathon, when I was good and drunk.

"Yeah, um, huh? You don't mean…?"

"I need you to go with me, Jake. I'll have my assistant send the clothes and a car will pick you up and bring you to the hotel. Please, I can't go alone."

I leaned back and took a deep breath. "Oh hey, I'd love to help ya out, but that's not my scene. Besides, the press would have a field day dredging up my shit. I'm doing better now, Cass, I really am. I'm in a good place - I'm working, taking care of Ma, all of it. I can't go back to all of that with you, not even for a few hours."

"Please, Jake, please." She looked so beautiful that it broke my heart. But I knew what Cassie Lane did to me.

"No."

———

But hours later, I couldn't get her off of my mind. My house still smelled like her perfume. All I wanted was to be near Cass again. Even if it destroyed me, sent me back to rehab, shit, even sent me back to jail, I couldn't stay away.

———

About Sam's Town, *Coming Soon from Sam JD Hunt:*

Cassidy Lane has it all—fame, money, and the perfect celebrity boyfriend. Until, that is, he dumps her right before the biggest award show of the year. She runs home to her mother, as she always does. "Make him jealous," her well-meaning mother advises. But with whom?

Jake Tanner never thought he'd see his high-school sweetheart, the now-famous actress Cassidy Lane, standing at the dilapidated door of his childhood home. He's even more shocked when he hears what she wants him to do…

Fooling the Hollywood elite is one thing, guarding their hearts from the love that threatens to destroy them is another. Can love prevail in the dark shadow of Sam's Town?

———

Stay tuned for more of Jake's story as well as other future installments of the hit series Sam's Town *from Sam JD Hunt.*

About the Author

Sam JD Hunt resides in Las Vegas with her husband as well as her two children.

When not writing, Hunt enjoys travel, community involvement, spending time with friends and family, and hiking. She spends her days writing and trying to answer the age-old question: is it too late for coffee or too early for wine?

facebook.com/SJDHunt

twitter.com/sjd_hunt

instagram.com/sjd_hunt

Also by Sam JD Hunt

Sam's Town Series:

REDEMPTION

SACRIFICE

Killing the King: Saints & Sinners Book One

The Thomas Hunt Series:

Roulette: Love Is A Losing Game

Blackjack: Wicked Game

Poker: Foolish Games

Deep: A Captive Tale

The Hunt for Eros

Dagger: American Fighter Pilot

Taken by Two

Torn from Two

Taken in Tahoe

Deeper: Capture of the Virgin Bride

Santino the Eternal

Gay for Pay

Be sure to follow Krsto's story in Rae B. Lake's *Condemn*, also available now in print and for Kindle.

Read all the extended stories from *CUFFED* and *PINCHED*, now available individually in ebook and paperback from the project's authors.

Including:

Dead or Alive by Janine Infante Bosco
- books2read.com/u/boajRL

Dead Reckoning by Gwyn McNamee
- books2read.com/DeadReckoningGM

Corrupt by Aubree Valentine - amzn.to/3CKNXyb

Duty by Elizabeth Knox - amzn.to/3m14Grd

Condemn by Rae B. Lake - books2read.com/u/4EKROl

Search & Find by Darlene Tallman - books2read.com/u/3Gwe1d

Hide & Seek by Liberty Parker - books2read.com/u/mdDGaW

The Weight of Honor by Kristine Allen
- books2read.com/u/bzdeEL

The Weight of Blood by M. Merin - books2read.com/u/4joA0D

Ground Zero by April Canavan - geni.us/GroundZero

Penalty Box by Casey Hagen - geni.us/PenaltyBox

Jaxson's Blue Moon by Cyndi Faria
- books2read.com/jaxsonsbluemoon

Cujo's Rampage by Khloe Wren
- books2read.com/CujosRampage

Cuff Linked by C.D. Gorri - books2read.com/cufflinked

Down in Flames by Elena Kincaid
- books2read.com/DownInFlames

Sinful Duty by Nicole Garcia - books2read.com/u/3nE7de

The Gamble by Nicole Banks - books2read.com/u/3LR6j7

Printed in the USA
CPSIA information can be obtained
at www.ICGtesting.com
LVHW050846030824
787272LV00033B/695